He pulled his ripcord. Something was wrong. He twisted, trying to see. His chute streamed out flat, not inflated. He swore to himself, more in exasperation than alarm. The ground was screaming up to meet him as he pulled the second ripcord, secure in the knowledge that soon he'd be bobbing below the safety of a square-shaped parachute.

But there was no reassuring shock of his weight yanked by the braking of an air-filled canopy. "Jesus! No!"

Milton Ryce's last conscious thought as he fell to earth was red rage. This couldn't be happening to him!

Visit

Bella Books

at

BellaBooks.com

or call our toll-free number

1-800-729-4992

FALL GUY

THE 16th DETECTIVE INSPECTOR
CAROL ASHTON MYSTERY

BY
CLAIRE McNAB

Bella
BOOKS

2004

Bella Books, Inc.
P.O. Box 10543
Tallahassee, FL 32302

Printed in the United States of America on acid-free paper
First Edition

Editor: Anna Chinappi
Cover designer: Bonnie Liss (Phoenix Graphics)

ISBN 1-59493-000-7

For Sheila

Acknowledgments

My thanks again to my truly excellent editor Anna Chinappi,
eagle-eyed proofreaders Judy Eda and Pamela Berard,
and assiduous typesetter Therese Szymanski.

Prologue

Milton Ryce tumbled gracefully out into the void, rejoicing in the exhilaration of free-falling. Spreading his arms, he had the illusion of flying, the earth wheeling beneath him, the sky his home.

Above, he caught sight of Verity Stuart's red suit as she exited the bright blue Leapers Anonymous plane. He laughed to himself. However many times Verity jumped, she would always be a conservative free-faller, pulling the ripcord far too soon. But this time he knew there'd be no reassuring tug of her parachute opening. Verity would panic, the stupid bitch. He wished there was some way a camera could catch her expression as she plummeted toward the unyielding ground.

She'd have wet herself by the time she activated her emergency chute. This time it'd work, of course. He hadn't tampered with it. "The joke's on you," he'd say, when he arrived shortly after her.

Verity would be babbling, hysterical, then mortified as she realized her humiliation. And with a bit of luck, Ted would have got close enough as she landed to catch every bit of her performance with his video camera.

Milton Ryce checked the altimeter on his wrist. Above him, Verity would be checking her altimeter, then deploying her useless main canopy. He chuckled again, then pulled his own ripcord. With any luck she'd plummet past him, her shriek lost in the howling of the wind, before her second chute released.

Something was wrong. He twisted, trying to see. His chute streamed out flat, not inflated. He swore to himself, more in exasperation than alarm. The ground was screaming up to meet him as he pulled the second ripcord, secure in the knowledge that soon he'd be bobbing below the safety of a square-shaped parachute.

But there was no reassuring shock of his weight yanked by the braking of an air-filled canopy. "Jesus! No!"

Milton Ryce's last conscious thought as he fell to earth, was red rage. This couldn't be happening to him!

Chapter One

"Right here, Inspector Ashton," said Sergeant Huffner. "He hit the ground somewhere between two hundred and three hundred kilometers an hour, they tell me." His tone of lugubrious satisfaction suited his heavily jowled, rectangular face.

Carol and Bourke examined the appreciable impression in the surface of the lightly grassed paddock. It was a beautiful and still Sunday afternoon. The azure sky was embellished by banks of fat white clouds. Overhead a hawk soared.

"You were first on the scene and secured the area?" Carol asked.

Huffner frowned, apparently examining Carol's question for hidden pitfalls. "I arrived at ten-forty yesterday morning, Inspector, about fifteen to twenty minutes after it happened. Got here as fast as I could, but we country cops have further to drive than you city types. Beat the ambulance by at least twenty-five minutes. They were rushing Mrs. Davy—six months pregnant with complications—to hospital when the call came in." With a sour smile he added, "When they did get here, wasn't much they could do, except scrape up what was left of him."

"They did a good job," Bourke remarked.

"You could say that, Sergeant," said Huffner, "although his jump suit pretty well held him together. Otherwise he'd have been splattered all over the area."

"I don't see any sign of body fluids," said Bourke.

"Well you wouldn't, would you? Look at the ground. It rained last night. We need rain badly here, but it was useless. A hard downpour, running off before the ground could absorb it."

"And there were no tarpaulins protecting the scene?"

Huffner's stolid features flushed at Carol's question. "No reason to suppose it was a suspicious death. I mean, this is a popular area for parachuting. I've seen enough of 'em hit the ground hard. There was some young woman a couple of months ago, flattened herself good and proper. They didn't send you out for that, did they?"

Carol felt a touch of sympathy for the country cop. There had been no reason for him to suspect Milton Ryce's death had been caused by anything other than a disastrous equipment malfunction.

A routine post-accident inspection by the Australian Parachute Federation had revealed that Ryce's parachute pack had been deliberately tampered with. What seemed misfortune now appeared to be deliberate, though whether it was murder or suicide had yet to be determined.

Every line of Huffner's stocky body showed truculent resentment. "I followed procedures. How was I supposed to know it was anything but an accident? Mr. Ryce did his skydiving all the time. Just by the law of averages, eventually something would go wrong."

Consternation suddenly filled his face as he looked past Carol and Bourke. "Oh, shit," he said, half under his breath.

They turned to see the source of his dismay. A bright red convertible was pulling up beside the gate. As they watched, a young woman leapt out of the car, flung open the gate and strode toward them.

"Who is it?" Carol asked.

"Rae Ryce. The daughter."

The young woman halted in front of them. She was dressed in black jeans and a scarlet, scoop-necked top. Her dark hair was slicked back. She had a diamond stud in one nostril, a row of gold rings in each ear. Carol thought she'd be attractive, if her face hadn't been clenched in a scowl.

"Where did he hit?"

Huffner made an awkward gesture, perhaps meaning to comfort her, but he withdrew his hand when she sent him a flat stare. He cleared his throat. "Rae, you shouldn't be here."

"I want to see where he died." She added mockingly, "It'll bring me closure."

Hands on hips, she surveyed the ground. Her gaze stopped at the depression. "Is that the place?" Her voice was as taut as her body.

Carol said, "It is, Ms. Ryce."

Rae Ryce glanced at Carol and Bourke. "And who are you?" she demanded.

"Police officers from Sydney," said Huffner. "There's nothing for you to see here, Rae. You should leave."

Rae's lip curled. "You think I should leave, do you, Sergeant Huffner?" Switching her attention to Carol and Bourke, she said, "Who's in charge?"

"I am, Ms. Ryce. Detective Inspector Carol Ashton. And this is Detective Sergeant Mark Bourke. I will have some questions for you. I'm sorry to have to ask them at this sad time."

"Sad time?" Rae Ryce threw her head back with a harsh laugh. "I'm pleased the bastard's dead!"

Huffner, scandalized, exclaimed, "You don't mean that! You're upset."

She cast him such a look of malevolence that he blinked. "I know exactly what I mean. I don't need you to tell me."

5

Carol was intrigued at palpable tension between the two. "I gather you know each other well."

Rae showed her teeth in an acid smile "Huffner here is Dad's right-hand man. Ask him. He'll tell you what great mates they are."

"Ms. Ryce," said Carol firmly, "I think you should be aware there's a possibility your father's death was not an accident. We are here to investigate the circumstances. I would appreciate your cooperation."

She seemed stunned. "Not an accident? You think someone killed him?"

Bourke said, "It's a possibility. So is suicide."

"Jesus." She put a hand to her mouth. "Are you sure it wasn't an accident?"

The young woman's shock appeared genuine, but Carol reserved judgment, having seen many guilty individuals put on Academy Award performances before. She said briskly, "We're not sure of anything yet. That's why we need to conduct interviews."

Rae Ryce shook her head violently. "No way. I can't answer any questions now. Later, maybe . . ."

"We *must* speak with you, Ms. Ryce. When will be convenient? Are you returning to Sydney today?"

Rae cupped her face in her hands for a moment, then looked up. She seemed to be fighting for control. "I'll be at the Hall," she said. "You can see me there, later this afternoon."

Carol watched her hurry toward her car, her previous confident stride now a rush to get away.

"How do you know Rae Ryce?" Bourke asked Huffner.

The sergeant raised his heavy shoulders. "You know how it is," he said. "Kids drive too fast, or make a bit of a commotion—just high spirits . . ." He paused, apparently for them to nod understandingly. When neither did, he went on, "Fact of the matter is, Rae's father had a private word to me. Asked if I'd keep an eye out. Make sure she didn't get into trouble." He shifted his feet uneasily. "Nothing I wouldn't do for any parent, you understand."

Carol caught Bourke's speculative look. They were both think-

6

ing the same thing: Sergeant Huffner had something to hide. It might be nothing more than ignoring some minor infraction by Rae Ryce or some other member of the family, but it could be worth checking out.

Obviously very keen to get on to a safer topic, Huffner said, "Inspector? You've got my detailed report—I sat up half the night writing it—but I suppose you'd like me to go through what I found when I arrived here yesterday."

"That would be helpful."

"Okay then." He swung around to point to the gate. "I get the call, and come straight here. Stop outside, where we're parked now. Here in the paddock, just inside the fence, are two four-wheel drives, both Land Rovers, latest models. There's a woman sobbing her heart out in the front seat of one. I find out later her name's Kymberly Watson. I never get anything out of her. She's too upset, and a bit later this doctor arrives and takes her away."

Carol, who'd scanned Huffner's report, said, "That would be Dr. Edmundson?"

"Yeah, Gilbert Edmundson. He gives me his card. Not a local. Never seen him before."

Carol was familiar with the name. Dr. Gilbert Edmundson ran a substance abuse clinic in Sydney called Inner Grace, the clientele of which was largely drawn from the famous and the seriously rich.

"And Dr. Edmundson also spoke with Milton Ryce's son?"

"Since you already know all this, why am I telling you again?" asked Huffner, obviously annoyed.

"I know it's tiresome," said Carol with a sympathetic smile, "but please walk us through it from the beginning."

He sighed heavily, but softened to say, "Okay, let's go to the gate and we'll take it from there."

As they followed the sergeant's hefty figure, Bourke said in an aside to Carol, "You're all blond charm today. Poor guy's putty in your hands."

Carol grinned. "I'm aging fast, Mark. Have to wring every little advantage out of my blond charm while I've still got it."

Ahead of them, Huffner had halted by the gate. "When I arrive, the Watson woman's here, sitting in a Land Rover. Ted Ryce, the son, comes up to me, says, 'There's been a dreadful accident.'"

"Did Kymberly Watson seem genuinely upset?" asked Bourke.

"She was a mess, weeping and wailing. Could have been an act, I suppose."

"And Ted Ryce?"

"He wasn't crying, if that's what you mean, but he looked pretty sick. Right about then, Dr. Edmundson turns up, takes a quick look at the Watson woman, then comes up to me and gives me his card. Says the woman's too upset to be interviewed, and that he's taking her with him for treatment."

"You didn't object?"

"Why would I, Inspector? There was no way I was going to get a statement out of her, the way she was."

"What then?" said Bourke.

Huffner swung around and began to retrace his steps toward the site of Ryce's violent death. "So I say to Ted to show me, and he starts walking this way. He's got a camera slung over his shoulder—the latest video camcorder—and I ask if he got a shot of the fall, and he looks even sicker, and says yes."

"You took possession of the camera?"

Huffner's face darkened. "Why would I do that?"

"For the coroner," said Carol mildly. "You knew there'd have to be an inquest into Ryce's death, accident or not."

"I told Ted to make sure he kept everything that was on it." Apparently feeling the need to justify himself further, Huffner went on, "What was there to see? Someone falling out of the sky? I don't know why you're concentrating on what happened down here." He pointed heavenward. "It's what happened up there that killed him."

"Someone observing the jump could be responsible," said Bourke.

Huffner mused on this. "Christ, that'd be cold," he said.

"Bloody cold. Watching someone step out of a plane, knowing a few moments later they're going to smash into the ground."

"In your report you mention there were two other witnesses, Verity Stuart and Ian McNamara."

"Yeah, they were the other two skydivers." He sent Carol an unexpected smile. "Landed rather more successfully than Ryce, I'd reckon."

Indicating a spot a short way from the depression the falling body had created, he went on, "Verity Stuart was crouched down a few meters away. She had on a red-and-blue jump suit, and her orange parachute was bundled up beside her. She was in a state, had thrown up all over the place. Couldn't get a word of sense out of her, except something about how *her* main parachute had malfunctioned, so I went to speak with McNamara. He was sort of standing sentry duty by the body. He had his head bent and could have been praying, for all I know."

It was news to Carol that there'd been another equipment malfunction. "Verity Stuart had a problem with her parachute? You didn't mention this before."

Huffner jutted his jaw. "I didn't think of it. Had my hands full with the fatality, didn't I? Kept me busy collecting everything to do with Ryce's parachute pack. Had my digital camera with me, so took a few shots first." He gave Carol a criticize-me-if-you-dare look. "I knew it'd be evidence for the inquest, and the APF would want to have a look, too."

"What happened to Verity Stuart's parachute?" Bourke wanted to know.

Huffner grimaced. "No idea."

Carol felt a pulse of irritation. "Locate it, Sergeant, as a matter of urgency."

He seemed about to demur, then said, "Come to think of it, Inspector, I believe the other guy, McNamara, bundled hers up and took it with his own parachute. I seem to remember seeing him dumping both into one of the Land Rovers. Then she got in, and they drove away."

"All the skydiving equipment used that day needs to be examined. The moment we finish here, Sergeant, I expect you to find out exactly where Ms. Stuart and Mr. McNamara's parachutes are."

Clearly taken aback at Carol's whiplash tone, Huffner gave a reluctant nod. "Right away."

"What was your impression of McNamara?" asked Bourke, his voice a good-cop contrast to Carol's brusque manner.

Clearly relieved to be off the subject of missing parachutes, Huffner said confidingly, "McNamara struck me as one of those no-panic, icy-control guys, know what I mean? He was the one who phoned the accident in. Just gave the location and what had happened. No 'Oh, my God' stuff or anything like it. It was the same when I spoke to him in person—cool as a cucumber."

"And he told you . . . ?"

"Not much. He'd been out of the plane first, did a free fall for half a minute or so, pulled his ripcord, and floated down, right on schedule. Then he looked up and saw someone's chute hadn't opened. A few moments later, Ryce hit. Instant death, of course. Then the other jumper, the woman, made it to the ground."

"He didn't mention any mid-air collision between the skydivers, or anything unusual?" Carol asked.

"He didn't mention anything, not that I had much time to question him," said Huffner. "About then the ambulance arrived, followed by the local APF guy. I left them to it. Got the witnesses out of the way and wrote down their particulars."

Since late yesterday afternoon, Carol had been on a crash course as far as the ins and out of skydiving were concerned, and had already found that the Australian Parachute Federation was the governing body of the sport. She'd spoken on the phone to Randall Schumacher of the APF, and been informed that the Civil Aviation Safety Authority set regulations for parachute jumping. He'd advised her to go online to the official APF site to get some overview of skydiving in Australia.

The regulations covered criteria for the type and standard of equipment. This included a requirement that all reserve parachutes must be inspected and repacked every six months by an APF licensed packer or rigger.

"I'd like to speak with the APF person who examined Ryce's gear," she said.

"If you like. He won't have anything to add."

"And we will need to interview any of the witnesses who have stayed in the area."

"Yeah, okay." Huffner was restive, glancing at his watch and then looking longingly in the direction of his vehicle.

"We're keeping you from something, Sergeant?" asked Carol.

"Look, Inspector, I've got a lot on my plate at the moment. We're not overstaffed here in Hash's Creek, you know. Have to make do with what we've got. And we're not accustomed to outside help."

Which meant, Carol thought, Huffner considered the city cops to have an easier time of it, and he resented Carol and Bourke walking in and taking over.

"You didn't take written statements from any of the witnesses?" asked Bourke.

"I reckon that's where you come in." His expression was full of injured defiance. "I made notes. Extensive notes. It was obvious to me most of them were too thrown by what had happened to be in any state to give a formal statement. Besides, the bloody media had got wind of the accident. While I was getting everyone's contact particulars, Constable Whistler, my second in command, called to say the station phone was ringing off the hook and reporters had started turning up asking questions."

Carol was accustomed to the sharks of the media scenting blood and precipitating a news frenzy. "Who alerted them?"

"Not me." Huffner gave a disgusted grunt. "They were here fast as flies to rotting meat. Whistler had hardly got off the phone when a couple of helicopters appeared heading this way. Knowing it was only a matter of time until bloody reporters arrived at the scene, I told everyone to get the hell out of it. I'd contact them later."

"Have you made any statement to the media?"

"Me? I'm just a country cop. I know when to keep my mouth shut." His expression of umbrage deepened. "We're not stupid here in the country, you know. It was obvious strings were going to be pulled and the head office would take over."

"And you got us," Bourke observed cheerfully.

"Yeah," said Huffner without enthusiasm. "I got you two."

Chapter Two

Hash's Creek was a three-hour drive from Sydney, but to Carol it seemed to be far more remote. On the map, the town's location had been indicated by an insignificant black dot in the wilderness, entirely bypassed by the red ribbons of major roads.

Late that morning, when she and Bourke had driven into Hash's Creek, the dot had turned out to be a small, undistinguished town with two pubs and three churches. The wide main street had angle parking on both sides, providing many more available spaces than seemed necessary for the sparse Sunday traffic. There was a rundown general store, a sad little restaurant obviously in desperate need of renovation, a rainbow-painted fish-and-chips shop, and a tiny garage with three petrol pumps seemingly ancient enough to be antiques.

Although the two Hash's Creek pubs looked very much alike, being two-storied wooden buildings with wide verandas on both floors, edged by carved wooden balustrades, the one in which

Carol and Bourke were staying—imaginatively called the Hash's Creek Hotel—sported a plaque claiming the building was subject to a preservation order because of its historic worth.

They had registered, dumped the sparse luggage each had brought in their rooms, then gone in search of the local police station, where they were to meet the officer in charge, Sergeant Huffner. The station was situated at the rear of Hash's Creek's rather grandiose red-brick town hall, which had an elaborate facade and an ornate clock tower. The time indicated was frozen at twelve sharp, which made it accurate twice a day, at midnight and midday.

The New South Wales Police Service divided the country areas of the state into districts. Although Sergeant Huffner and his subordinate, Constable Whistler, answered to the district authorities, in practice they were relatively autonomous, and would be expected to handle most crime problems without outside assistance.

Milton Ryce's death had been a very definite exception to the rule. Even though it was the weekend, in Sydney the news on Saturday that the businessman's demise might not have come about by sheer bad luck had caused an immediate flurry of activity in political and social circles. Carol had been called in to the Commissioner's office from a cricket match where she'd been watching her son play for his school team. She found herself dispatched to Hash's Creek with instructions from the Commissioner to "get to the bottom of it, as quickly and neatly as you can."

It seemed obvious to her that some individuals in high places had skeletons they'd rather not have see the light of day. Carol had asked the obvious questions, hoping to gain insights that might help her inquiries, but had harvested a crop of generalizations and assurances she had been chosen to lead the investigation because of her skills in handling the media and her record of bringing high-profile cases to satisfactory conclusions.

Starting their Sunday morning drive to Hash's Creek, she and Mark Bourke had laughed over this last laudatory comment.

"A satisfactory conclusion," said Bourke, "means any political damage is contained and the ravenous media hordes are deflected onto something else."

"You're becoming deeply cynical," said Carol with mock disapproval. "Where's the sunny, clear-eyed cop I used to know?"

"Thinking of going for promotion. You've inspired me."

Delighted, she said, "Mark, that's wonderful. You know I'll do anything I can to help."

"By the way, Anne's working hard on making sergeant."

In her mind's eye, Carol could see Anne Newsome's animated, intelligent face. Somewhat of a protege of Carol's, the young constable was one of the most promising young officers Carol had encountered during her career. "That's good news. Anne's got the potential to go a long way."

"Did you know she belongs to a skydiving club?"

"Anne does? She's never mentioned it."

"She was telling me about it last week. You know how sporty she is? This is one of her new enthusiasms." Bourke grinned over at Carol. "May have something to do with her latest boyfriend. He's into skydiving in a big way."

They had chatted on about the office politics for a while, then fallen silent. With Bourke driving, Carol could sit back and enjoy the scenery. Years of drought had parched the land, but it still had a stubborn, tenacious beauty. Brown grass filled the paddocks. The gray-green of eucalyptus gums crowded the hills. Occasional slashes of green indicated the paths of streams. The blue arch of sky went on and on into infinity.

Carol was flooded with an unaccustomed serenity, a mood that was abruptly broken by Bourke saying, "Leota's left, hasn't she?"

"Yes. Last week."

He glanced over at her. "Regrets?"

She kept her eyes on the road unwinding before them. "Not a topic for discussion."

"Okay."

When she looked across at him, his blunt-featured face was

closed, blank. She felt a stab of contrition. He was more to her than just a colleague. And he'd asked as a friend, not out of idle curiosity. He and Pat, his wife, had met Leota several times. Bourke had got on well with the FBI agent, trading stories about life in their respective law enforcement trenches.

Although never discussed between them, Carol knew he'd realized the depth of her feelings for Leota Woolfe. When Leota, on assignment to Australia as an expert on counter-terrorism, had told Carol she was to be recalled to the States, she'd asked Carol to go with her.

Carol had felt agonizingly pulled two ways: on one side her country and her career, on the other Leota and all the warmth and love she brought to their growing relationship. It was a struggle to make a decision. Carol wasn't altogether sure her choice not to go was irrevocable. Leota's last words to her still rang in Carol's ears: "Honey, it isn't over. Don't ever think it is."

For the rest of the trip, the easeful atmosphere had evaporated. She and Bourke spoke little, and finally, as they reached the signpost indicating Hash's Creek was only a kilometer away, she'd said, "Mark, I'm sorry. It's too soon for me to talk about it. I hope you understand."

"I shouldn't have intruded."

"It's not that. I haven't really discussed Leota with Aunt Sarah, and she's a lot more persistent than you will ever be."

Bourke had grinned. "Too true. You'd be the only one I can think of who could resist your aunt. She'd put the KGB to shame."

Milton Ryce had a luxurious mansion in Turramurra, one of Sydney's prestigious northern suburbs. He also had a country estate outside Hash's Creek. Before they left the site of Ryce's death, Sergeant Huffner took a district map from his glove box and painstakingly marked the route to Ryce Hall.

It was here that Rae Ryce had said she was going. Huffner remarked they'd likely find her brother there, too. In addition, he recommended they speak with Neville Bendix, Ryce's pilot, who'd been flying the plane when the tragedy occurred.

Prior to leaving Sydney, Bourke had done some quick research on the Ryce family. He filled Carol in on the details as they followed Huffner's directions to the Hall.

"Milton Ryce was on his third wife when he died. The first one, Marion, is the mother of his two children, Ted and Rae. They're fraternal twins, both in their mid-twenties. The marriage was rocky, but before Marion could divorce him, she died in a car accident."

"Anything suspicious about it, Mark?"

He shook his head. "Just your standard fatal car crash. Lost control on a corner and rolled it. Ryce didn't grieve for long—within a couple of months he'd married a Tiffany Maxwell. She lasted three years. Very acrimonious divorce, particularly as there was a prenuptial agreement that pretty well assured Tiffany got peanuts. Six months later he married his present wife, Deanna Lustgarten. The word is she was preparing to divorce him too, but a defective parachute has saved her the trouble."

As Bourke negotiated the gravel entrance road to Ryce Hall, Carol's mobile phone rang. It was Huffner with the news that he'd located Verity Stuart and Ian McNamara's parachutes. "I've just spoken to McNamara. He and the Stuart woman went back to Sydney last night, but before they left, they dumped the chutes in the hangar at Ryce's private airfield."

Carol relayed this information to Bourke as they neared the house. Confounding her expectations, the Ryce country home was rather austere. There was an ordinary cattle grid at the entrance and the fencing was basic, being several strands of barbed wire strung tight between steel posts. A cardboard sign, neatly printed, announced: NO INTERVIEWS. NO STATEMENTS. ALL TRESPASSERS WILL BE PROSECUTED.

The house itself was a long, low, wooden building surrounded by native trees. Its wooden walls were a dull brown, and it blended into the landscape as though part of it.

Carol had called ahead, speaking with a cool-voiced man with a clipped English accent, who'd introduced himself as a friend of the family. "Larry Frobisher, Inspector Ashton. I imagine you'll be wanting to arrange an interview with Ted. Yes?"

Frobisher introduced himself in person when he opened the front door. He was a petite man, with tiny hands and feet and a head of thick, springy hair emphasizing the impression that his skull was a shade too large for his body. Looking up at Carol, he revealed small, sharp teeth in a quick smile. He had on what Carol privately thought of as "English country clothes"—tailored slacks, a fine linen shirt casually open at the throat, and a tweed jacket with leather patches on the elbows.

Frobisher waved away Carol's attempt to show her identification. "You've a famous face, Inspector Ashton, so naturally I recognized you immediately." He gave Bourke an appraising glance. "But I'm afraid I don't know . . ."

"Detective Sergeant Mark Bourke," said Carol.

Frobisher stood aside to allow them to enter. He led them to a sitting room full of comfortable furniture. The room looked well lived in, as if it were in constant use. It was hot outside, but the air-conditioning kept the room cool, and there was a wood fire burning in the fireplace. The mantel above was lined with various family photographs. A quick glance gave Carol the impression Milton Ryce appeared in most of them.

The entrepreneur had had a lean, whippet-like body, an ascetic face, and a confrontational stance. In most of the photographs his head was thrust forward in clenched-jaw aggression.

As soon as they were seated, Frobisher said to Carol, "I hear on the grapevine that you are soon to be Detective *Chief* Inspector Ashton. May I be the first to congratulate you on your well-deserved promotion."

"May I ask where you obtained that information?"

"I have my sources, Inspector Ashton." His expression smug, he repeated, "I have my sources."

"Mr. Larry Frobisher?" said Bourke. "Would that be *Lawrence* Frobisher?"

The little man gave an odd little duck of his head. "It would be. To my friends, I'm Larry, of course."

"You have an online gossip column, the Lawrence Frobisher Report."

Frobisher's face darkened. Turning to Carol, he said, "May I point out your Sergeant is careless with words. Very careless. The Frobisher Report is an online column analogous to the commentary one might find in a reputable news magazine." He shot a look of pure dislike in Bourke's direction. "It is true I have achieved a certain notoriety, mainly because of the accuracy of the information I release, however the Frobisher Report is not and never will be a gossip column. It is a far more substantial contribution to journalism than that."

"You're having yourself on, Larry," said a lazy voice from the doorway. "Your blog's successful because it's sensational. Go on, admit it."

Frobisher bounced to his feet. "May I present Theodore Ryce, better known as Ted."

Ted Ryce, lanky and awkward, slouched into the room. He wore grubby jeans and a once white T-shirt. In looks he resembled his father, but where Milton Ryce's face had been angles and hard bone under flesh, Ted Ryce had softer, rounder features. His hair was much longer, but he was, Carol thought, like a slightly out of focus likeness of his parent.

Carol rose to shake the young man's hand, as Frobisher continued, "Ted, this blond beauty is, astonishingly, a police officer, to wit, Inspector Carol Ashton."

Bourke, ignored by Frobisher, introduced himself.

"I'll leave you to it," said Frobisher. "Call me if you need me."

"I won't need you." Ted Ryce flung himself into the nearest lounge chair and swung his feet over an arm so his unlaced running shoes dangled.

"Our deepest sympathies for your loss," said Carol.

Ted didn't meet her eyes. "The local cop knows everything about the accident," he drawled. "Nothing I can add. My dad just fell out of the sky. End of story."

"I'm afraid there's more to it than that."

Ted Ryce's head jerked up. "What's that supposed to mean?"

"Have you spoken with your sister?" Carol asked.

"Rae? No. She went back to Sydney on Friday night after a bit of an argument with Dad. Haven't been able to raise her on her cell phone. She may not even know Dad's dead."

"She knows," said Bourke. "Your sister was at the site with us this afternoon. She was obviously very shaken by the possibility your father's death was not an accident. She left, saying she was coming here."

Ted flashed a surprisingly sweet smile. "Haven't seen her, but that's Rae for you," he said indulgently. "She changes her mind like the wind."

"What was the argument on Friday night about?" Carol asked.

He shrugged. "Nothing serious. Same old, same old. Rae and Dad didn't get on, basically. Never have."

"We need to locate your sister as a matter of urgency," Carol said. "It's essential we speak to everyone who was close to your father."

Ted gave her a long stare, then looked away. "Heard some wild story about Dad's parachute being tampered with. Don't believe it. Dad was scrupulous. Checked his equipment before every jump."

"Who told you about the possible tampering?"

He flicked a glance at her. "Bush telegraph. No one can keep a secret long in Hash's Creek." He made a face. "I suppose that means the bloody reporters will be back here again."

"What do you think happened?" asked Bourke, flipping open his notebook.

"Some freak thing. You make more than a thousand jumps, and once, just once, something goes wrong. That's the way it is."

Carol contemplated the young man's sprawled figure. He

seemed relaxed, although one foot was moving in a jerky rhythm. If he was grieving, he was hiding it well. In itself, this lack of obvious anguish didn't necessarily mean anything. Carol knew from long experience how people dealt with sorrow in different ways.

She glanced over at Bourke, who took up the questioning. "Do you parachute yourself, Mr. Ryce?"

"Yeah. I'm almost as keen as Dad."

"But you weren't up in the plane yesterday."

"I was relegated to ground transport."

Picking up on his sardonic tone, Bourke smiled sympathetically. "Pretty boring, eh?"

Ted shrugged, then yawned widely. "I didn't get much sleep last night. I'm sure you'll understand why. I'd appreciate it if we kept this short." He swung his feet around to place them on the floor. Obviously about to stand, he said, "Basically there's nothing I can tell you that you don't already know."

Carol said, "If your father's death wasn't an accident—"

"Then it was murder or suicide." His tone was matter-of-fact.

"Those would seem to be the alternatives."

"Suicide's out," said Ted Ryce with conviction. "Dad wouldn't kill himself under any circumstances."

"Who would wish him harm?"

Ryce gave an incredulous laugh. "You're kidding me, right? My father had enemies coming out of the woodwork. He could be a real bastard. Most people hated him."

"Did you?" Bourke inquired.

With a grim smile, Ted Ryce said, "I was just about the only exception. We got on like a house on fire. Ask my stepmother. She'll tell you I'm a chip off the old block. Dad could see himself in me, and he liked that."

Carol raised her eyebrows. "Does that mean you favor practical jokes, Mr. Ryce?"

"Love 'em. Since I was a kid I've got a kick out of sending people up."

Carol kept her expression neutral. She'd always disliked practi-

21

cal jokes, and Milton Ryce had been an odious exponent, with the money and time to set up elaborate scenarios to humble and embarrass as many as possible. Carol had long considered him a detestable individual who'd tied up police resources on numerous occasions, and at least once indirectly been the cause of serious injury when he'd set up a hoax involving a fake faith healer.

At a well-publicized public meeting the healer could be seen touching apparently blind children, who suddenly screamed that they could see, and taking the hands of paralyzed individuals, who then rose from their wheelchairs and walked.

In the hysterical mobbing of the stage that followed, several in the audience were injured. Later, when the hoax was revealed, Milton Ryce refused to take any responsibility for those hurt in the crush, remarking that they were victims of their own gullibility.

Ryce had always gone to great trouble to make filmed records of his exploits, which he'd display widely to the extreme discomfort of those he'd ridiculed. And he didn't stick to anonymous members of the public, but drew many of his victims from society and sports circles, as well as business leaders with whom his electronics company dealt with day to day.

Ryce had been sued often, but mostly unsuccessfully, as his sizable fortune enabled him to buy the very best legal representation available. In his career as joker he'd been declared a public nuisance, had paid fines for various trespassing offenses and for endangering the public with his stunts. None of this discouraged him in his enthusiasm for hoaxes and extravagant practical jokes.

"Could his accident have been a practical joke gone wrong?" Carol asked.

Ted shook his head emphatically. "No way. Dad played jokes on others. He was too smart to ever let anyone do it back to him."

Bourke said, "We've been told Verity Stuart also had trouble with her parachute."

With more animation than he'd shown before, Milton's bereaved son exclaimed, "She sure did! It would have been a hoot, except for Dad dying."

"A hoot?"

"It was a setup, Inspector Ashton. Dad had me waiting on the ground with a camcorder to catch Verity's hysterics when she landed."

Sounding suitably incredulous, Bourke said, "Are you saying that your father tampered with this woman's parachute?"

He nodded agreeably. "That's what I'm saying. It was just a bit of fun. Verity's a panic merchant. When her chute didn't open, we knew she'd wet herself. By the time she thought to pull the emergency ripcord, she'd be screaming her head off."

Bourke looked over at Carol with a do-you-believe-this-guy look, then said to Ted Ryce, "And you and your father thought this was funny? To terrify someone?"

"Oh, yeah. Small stuff though. What did you think of the UFO hoax a couple of weeks ago? It was Dad's idea, but I worked on it with him. Too much! We sucked in the TV networks. Were their faces red when we showed them up. What a laugh."

"It would assist our investigations if we could take temporary possession of the camcorder and the video you shot yesterday." Carol didn't add that if he failed to cooperate, she'd serve a warrant on him.

"It's not video, it's a DVD." He got to his feet. "I'll get it for you, as long as you give me a receipt."

When he'd left the room, Bourke said quietly to Carol, "Really broken up about his father's death, isn't he?"

"Perhaps he's putting on a brave front."

Bourke snorted at this. "He doesn't give a brass razoo. I'm starting to wonder what Milton Ryce's last will and testament contains."

"I can tell you that, Sergeant," said a voice from the doorway. Laden with a heavy tray that emphasized his slight frame, Larry Frobisher came into the room. "I thought you'd appreciate refreshments."

Setting the tray down on a coffee table, he continued, "Apart from a bequest to a children's charity, the major part of Milton's estate goes to his family. His wife, Deanna, gets half: Ted and Rae receive a quarter each."

"May I ask how you know this?" said Carol, accepting the proffered delicate china cup. The aroma of high-quality coffee tickled her nose.

"Coffee for you, too, Sergeant?" Frobisher passed over another elegant cup to Bourke, saying, "Milton discussed the whole issue with me recently. He was intending to change his will. His marriage was in trouble, and I advised him to wait until he and Deanna had decided whether the relationship could be saved."

"If rumors are to be believed," said Bourke, "it seems it couldn't be saved. I'd heard a divorce was in the offing."

Frobisher beamed at him. "So you've been checking out my Web site, have you? I broke the news in the Lawrence Frobisher Report last week." His smile faded. "Of course, the media picked the story up and ran with it. Lazy bastards. They use my material, but give me attribution? No way!"

"So it wasn't you who alerted the media that Milton Ryce had died in a skydiving accident?"

"It certainly wasn't me, Inspector. I admit, however, as soon as I heard what happened, I posted the news of Milton's death on my Web site. It's conceivable a journalist saw it almost immediately."

With a vexed expression, he went on, "Unfortunately I wasn't first with the story about the cut lines on Milton's parachute. I've got it up on the Web site, but it's not a scoop. Bloody annoying."

"Do you have any idea who alerted the media it wasn't an accident?"

"Not a clue, Inspector, but strictly between us, I wouldn't put it past Huffner. He's got spotter's fees in the past."

"You have evidence?"

Frobisher grinned. "Sure. I paid the sergeant a few dollars myself for a tip. At a party a few months ago, Basil Clement king-hit Gilbert Edmundson, society doctor to the stars. Near broke his jaw. I'm sure you're aware how the gossip columns love to dish the dirt on Basil Clement. I made a nice profit on that item."

"Have you sold items about Milton Ryce, too?"

Outrage filled the little man's face. "Bite the hand that feeds me, Inspector? Do I look that stupid?"

"I wasn't implying you were stupid, Mr. Frobisher. You could have provided tips anonymously."

"One soon learned not to cross Milton in any way. The slightest hint of disloyalty, and he would turn on you like a rabid dog."

"Picturesque," murmured Bourke.

Frobisher smiled, his good humor restored. "Picturesque, Sergeant, but oh so accurate. Milton was an implacable enemy." He picked up a plate from the tray. "Scones, anyone? I have whipped cream and homemade strawberry jam."

Carol, to whom breakfast was a distant early morning memory, accepted the offer with alacrity. "This is very kind of you, Mr. Frobisher."

"Not at all, Inspector." He fished in his jacket pocket and came out with a business card. "I'd appreciate it if you'd contact me with any details you feel you can share. I'd particularly favor exclusive information."

Faintly amused, Carol took the card. "Bribery by scones," she remarked.

Frobisher tucked up his shoulders and ducked his head in a gesture Carol decided was a characteristic one. "Whatever it takes," he said with a smile. "May I assure you I never reveal my sources, so nothing will be traced back to you."

"I'm afraid—" Carol began.

"Never say never!" Frobisher exclaimed. "There may be times when it will be mutually advantageous for us to exchange information."

Bourke, who'd helped himself to a scone, washed it down with a gulp of coffee. "Speaking of information, a Kymberly Watson was at the scene yesterday when Mr. Ryce died. She left with Dr. Edmundson, who told the police officer in attendance she was too upset to be interviewed. We know Dr. Edmundson has returned to Sydney, but we haven't been able to locate Ms. Watson, and I wonder if you might know where she is."

"Kym? She's Milton's latest mistress."

"Latest?" said Carol, raising her eyebrows.

"Hell, yes. Milton had a string of them." He smirked. "Faithful in his way, though. Only one at a time."

"Do you have names?"

"Don't worry about it, Inspector. Not one would have a motive to kill him. When Milton got tired of a woman, he'd invariably give her a nice cash settlement. Oh, and a stringent nondisclosure agreement to sign, of course."

"How long has Ms. Watson been in favor?" asked Bourke.

"A few months. Milton set her up in a harborside flat in Sydney. Poor Kym will be out of there soon—she can't afford the rent herself. She had her sights set on being the fourth Mrs. Ryce, though I warned her it was hopeless. And even if he did marry her, none of his wives ever got any money out of him." Frobisher suddenly snickered. "Except Deanna, of course, and Milton had to be splattered all over a paddock for that to be a possibility."

"We have Ms. Watson's address in Sydney," said Bourke, "but apparently she hasn't returned home."

"You've been looking in the wrong place," Frobisher said. "She's staying here, if you want to see her."

He paused, then added with a sardonic smile, "I believe you'll find Kym simultaneously grieving and working on her tan."

Chapter Three

The swimming pool was situated at the rear of the house. As Frobisher led them down a long hallway, he gave a running commentary. "Ryce Hall is rather larger than it appears from the front. The building is constructed in the shape of a T, with a separate wing containing guest suites jutting past the swimming pool. In fact, I have my own suite there for my exclusive use."

"You were a close friend of Mr. Ryce's?"

Carol's question elicited a sardonic smile. "Milton didn't have close *friends*. I'd call myself an associate of his."

"You mean a partner?" Carol asked.

Frobisher chuckled. "More an accomplice. Milton loved to involve a small circle of people, something like a project team, when he planned his more spectacular stunts. He would choose one of us as project manager, responsible for setting the thing up and making sure it worked."

"This project manager role," said Bourke, "was it a paid position?"

"How sharp you are, Sergeant Bourke. It was indeed paid—excessively well paid. I wouldn't waste my time, without sufficient remuneration, I assure you."

"Would you name a recent practical joke with which you were involved?"

Frobisher shook his head. "I'm afraid not, Inspector. I signed a confidentiality agreement. I don't know if it's still in force, but until I get legal advice, I'm saying nothing." In an obvious change of subject, he gestured to a door they were passing, saying, "That's the music room, grand piano and all. Merely for show. Pitifully, Milton was totally tone deaf."

Carol had already noticed with amusement that beside each door an elegantly lettered plate announced the use for each room. She halted by one reading WAR ROOM. "What's this one?"

Frobisher threw the door open. "Have a look for yourselves."

"Wow," said Bourke, impressed. "This setup must be worth a fortune."

Model soldiers were arrayed on meticulously landscaped battlefields. When they stepped closer, Carol could see each little figure, uniform included, was painstakingly rendered with fine details. Some were in modern garb, but most depicted battles long ago, when soldiers wearing bright colors marched in formation to war, accompanied by the sound of drums and fifes.

"When not hatching plans to humiliate someone or jumping out of planes, Milton spent his time here, fighting battles with toy soldiers." Frobisher almost sneered. "Disconcerting hobby for a grown man, don't you think?"

Without waiting for a reply, he turned on his heel and exited the room, as if, Carol thought, he found himself uncomfortable to be there.

Carol and Bourke followed his slight figure through a spacious kitchen, where a middle-aged woman was preparing food, and into a cheerful, light-filled room, furnished with four brown leather booths with yellow Formica tables. "Everyone eats breakfast here," said Frobisher. He wrinkled his nose. "It's a meal I always avoid."

"What's the staffing here at Ryce Hall?"

28

Frobisher jerked his head in the direction of the kitchen. "Polly Treeve's been on the payroll for years. Practically one of the family. Lives in, runs the household, does all the cooking. She hires field hands, gardeners, all those sort of people, as needed. She's a treasure. Wouldn't mind employing her, myself."

Sliding glass doors led to a patio edged by trellises laden with brightly flowering vines. On the other side was the soothing blue-green of a crescent-shaped pool surrounded by palms and tree ferns. One of the white pool lounges had been positioned in full sunlight, and on it reclined an unmistakably female figure in a brief pink bikini.

"There's Kym, soaking up the sun like a lizard. Naturally she disregards warnings about the deleterious effects of sunlight upon the skin."

Frobisher left them with the promise that he would drive them to the airfield when they were ready. "It'd be easier than explaining the route to you."

"We'll follow you in our car," said Carol, not wanting to give Larry Frobisher any opportunity to make an excuse to enter Neville Bendix's house while she and Bourke were interviewing the pilot.

A shade of irritation crossed Frobisher's face. "Suit yourself."

Carol and Bourke had just stepped from the chilly air-conditioning of the house into the brassy heat of the patio, when Ted Ryce caught up with them. "Here's the camcorder," he said, shoving it into Carol's hands. "I'll get it back, won't I?"

As Bourke scribbled him a receipt, Carol said, "We'll return it as soon as we've determined if the material you shot is relevant to our investigation."

"You'll keep it secure? I've heard stories of cops selling footage like this to TV stations."

Annoyed at the implied criticism, Carol said coldly, "That won't happen, Mr. Ryce."

He squinted past her into the bright afternoon light. "Going to interview Kym, are you?"

"It's necessary to talk with all witnesses," said Carol blandly.

"Was Ms. Watson near you when your father jumped from the plane?"

"Yeah, right next to me. She was all dressed up and ready to pick up Dad after the jump and go on to a lunch somewhere. Dunno where. I wasn't interested enough to ask. She kept checking her watch and complaining they'd be late. Anyway, that's why she didn't go up yesterday, although she's a keen skydiver. That's how Dad met her in the first place."

"Mr. Frobisher intimated that Ms. Watson had a very close relationship with your father."

Ted Ryce stifled a snort of laughter. "How delicate of you, Inspector! They were lovers."

"And your stepmother . . . ?" said Bourke.

"Knew about the affair? Of course. That's why Deanna won't come up here anymore. She doesn't want to run the chance of meeting Kym face-to-face."

"We've heard divorce a possibility," Carol said.

"Dad was pushing for one. Deanna was dragging her feet. She'd been dumb enough to sign a prenuptial agreement. *Bad* idea. If she and Dad parted ways, she wasn't due to get much in the way of money."

He added cheerily, "Dad dying suddenly like this cancels out the prenup altogether. So, since Deanna's still legally married to him, my stepmother gets half his estate. Gives her a humungous motive, doesn't it?"

As Ted turned to go, Bourke said, "Mr. Ryce? We understand the skydiving equipment Ms. Stuart and Mr. McNamara used has been left at the airfield. We'd appreciate your permission to take the packs for examination."

"I've told you what you'll find—Verity's main parachute inoperative, but everything else working perfectly."

"I imagine you'll be requiring another receipt," said Carol dryly.

"If it isn't too much trouble. You can give it to Bendix."

A few moments later, as they moved into the full glare of the

30

unforgiving afternoon, Bourke said to Carol, "I reckon that young man's got an excellent motive himself. If he can persuade us his stepmother killed his father, then an educated guess says the bulk of the estate is divided between him and his sister."

"That gives Rae Ryce a nice motive, too."

"A brother and sister act," said Bourke, "keeping it all in the family. How's that for a scenario?"

"They can join the queue, Mark. I have a feeling before we're finished, the number of suspects will be daunting."

Kymberly Watson sat up and took off her sunglasses as Carol and Bourke approached. Carol thought she was the archetype of a rich man's mistress. A blue-eyed blond, her hair cascaded over her shoulders in artful disarray. She wore a very brief pink bikini. She had quite spectacular breasts, but the rest of her was so alarmingly thin that Carol had the fancy a firm hug would probably crack a rib or two.

Sergeant Huffner had described Kymberly Watson as weeping and wailing, but today she appeared all cried out. Her face, obviously pretty under better circumstances, was blotchy and swollen, but her eyes were dry and her manner calm.

"Call me Kym," she said in a high, piping voice, when Carol made the introductions.

"We're sorry to intrude at such a sad time," Carol said. "Unfortunately we need to speak to everyone who witnessed the tragedy."

"Milton was everything to me," Kym announced. "Everything." Her lips trembled. "And I saw him falling, falling . . . I screamed for him to open his chute, but still he fell . . ."

"A horrible experience," said Bourke sympathetically, taking out his notebook.

She turned her blue eyes on him. "Yes," she breathed, "horrible. No, worse than horrible. Devastating. You can't imagine how it feels to see someone you love die like that." She glanced at his notebook. "You're taking this down?" She seemed more pleased than surprised.

Bourke smiled. "Standard practice."

"I've never been questioned by the police before." Her face crumpled. "And to think it's because I saw Milton die . . ."

"Of course you were shocked and upset by the tragedy," said Carol. "Was that why you called Dr. Edmundson?"

"Gilbert? I didn't call him, Ian McNamara did. Gilbert was staying here at Ryce Hall, but he wasn't interested in skydiving, so he didn't come with us yesterday morning."

"I believe you and Mr. Ryce had a luncheon date."

Kym, recovered from her spasm of grief, said with some vivacity, "With the Clement brothers. You've heard of Basil Clement, I'm sure. Such a nice man. His brother Morris isn't nearly so well known. Anyway, they've got a country house nearby, and Milton and I were going there afterwards. I was so looking forward to it."

The mention of the luncheon revived her misery. She put a hand over her eyes, murmuring in a tragic tone, "But we never made it."

After a pause, during which Carol and Bourke exchanged wry glances, Kym Watson perked up enough to say, "At least Milton didn't suffer. Gilbert said he wouldn't have felt anything." She frowned. "Something about his speed at impact being faster than nerve impulses could travel."

"That must be a comfort," said Bourke, his face grave.

Carol positioned herself to take advantage of the sparse shade thrown by a spindly palm. "I gather you're quite expert in skydiving yourself," she said.

"It's something Milton and I shared. It's as close to flying as you can get, you know. Freefalling . . . it's just wonderful."

She tugged pensively at a curl of her hair. "You natural?" she said to Carol.

"I beg your pardon?"

"Your blond hair."

"Oh. Yes."

Kymberly Watson gave a discontented sigh. "Lucky you," she said. "Mine needs a little help . . . Let's face it, a *lot* of help."

Carol saw Bourke's lips curve slightly, but he sounded very serious as he said, "We're investigating how Mr. Ryce died, Ms. Watson."

"Kym," she said. "Forget the Ms. Watson stuff. And what's there to investigate? Both of Milton's parachutes failed. That's what went wrong."

"The question is, why did both malfunction?" said Bourke.

She gave Bourke a wide-eyed stare. "You can't think someone deliberately—" She broke off to shake her head. "No, it's not possible."

The woman was being disingenuous, Carol thought. Ryce's son had heard the rumors that his father's death hadn't been accidental. So had Larry Frobisher. It was hard to believe Kymberly Watson hadn't known about them, too.

"Mr. Ryce packed his own parachutes?" Carol asked.

"We're both qualified to do that. If you're going to take a sport seriously, then you learn every last detail." She gave Carol a shrewd look. "Okay, Inspector, you're going to ask about the equipment Milton used yesterday. The same as always, he packed it himself."

"You saw him do it?"

"No, of course not, but I know it was his routine."

"Air force experts are examining the parachutes," said Carol. "If they confirm there was deliberate tampering—"

"I can't help you!" Kym Watson got to her feet, then shuddered, as if touched by something cold. "I didn't get on the plane, or help load anything into it. It must be obvious to you I had everything to lose and nothing to gain from Milton's death."

She slowly sat down on the lounge again. "Sorry for that. Larry said I'd automatically be a suspect, being so close to Milton." She looked at Carol and Bourke with a pleading expression. "With Milton gone, I'll be forced to move out of my apartment within the month. Does that sound like I'd want him dead? Heaven knows, there must be others with real reasons to wish him harm."

"We have no suspects as yet," said Carol, "although we're aware

Mr. Ryce had enemies. For example, the many victims of his practical jokes."

"Inspector, they were *jokes*." She spread her hands. "I mean, if you can't laugh at yourself . . ."

"Some people don't find being humiliated in public all that amusing," Bourke observed.

"Some people just don't have a sense of humor."

"We'd appreciate any information you can give us," Carol said. "Did Mr. Ryce mention any threats he might have received recently?"

"Milton never paid any attention to what anyone said, so he wouldn't bother repeating anything like that to me." She leaned forward confidingly. "If I were you, I'd take a good long look at Milton's wife. Deanna's capable of anything."

"Why do you say she's capable of anything?"

Kymberly bestowed a sunny smile on Carol. "Oh, I don't know," she said. "Could be because in the past she killed somebody . . ."

"Deanna Ryce is going to be an interesting interview," said Carol as they made their way back to the house.

"Kymberly Watson would certainly like us to put Ryce's wife at the top of the list," said Bourke. "Here's betting Deanna Ryce returns the favor, and accuses the beautiful Kym."

In the kitchen, the housekeeper, Polly Treeve, was seated at a table, shelling peas. Looking at the pile of crisp green pods, Carol was suddenly transported back to her childhood. She'd spent summer holidays in the Blue Mountains, staying with her aunt and uncle. Countless times she'd helped Aunt Sarah shell peas from the garden. Every now and then Carol would cram the contents of a pod into her mouth, until Aunt Sarah would protest there wouldn't be enough for dinner.

Seeing them enter the kitchen, Polly Treeve got to her feet, wiping her hands on her apron. Then she waited stoically for Carol to speak.

"Ms. Treeve? I'm Detective Inspector Carol Ashton, and this is Detective Sergeant Mark Bourke. I wonder if we could ask you a few questions?"

"If you like."

She was the resilient, hard-to-fool type, Carol decided. The housekeeper was extremely thin and below average height, but there was no impression of frailty in her stance or in her direct gaze and firm mouth. Her graying hair was pulled back in a no-nonsense bun, and the only jewelry she wore was a plain, stainless steel watch and a wedding ring worn to a thin band of gold.

"You've been with Mr. Ryce for some time, I believe?" Carol said.

"Thirty years."

"How long have you been here at Hash's Creek?"

"Almost five years."

"And before Hash's Creek?"

"Different places. Mainly Sydney."

Bourke sent Carol an amused glance. She knew what he'd be thinking: this was a blood-out-of-a-stone interviewee. He said, "You must find the work rewarding, as you've stayed with the same employer so long."

"Can't complain."

"We're investigating Mr. Ryce's death."

"Sergeant Huffner's already seen me. I told him I know nothing about it."

"We're investigating it as a suspicious death," said Carol.

Polly Treeve nodded, but remained silent.

"Can you think of anyone who would want to harm him?"

Carol's question produced a wintry smile. "Mr. Ryce had more enemies than friends," she said. "It was his way."

"Can you think of anyone in particular?"

Polly Treeve gave her a long stare. "Not offhand."

A few more questions, and Carol silently admitted defeat. After they'd left the kitchen, she said to Bourke, "Mark, this needs a touch of your masculine charisma."

"Charisma, is it?" he said with a snort of laughter. "You're just sweet-talking me."

"You'll have to pay Polly a visit by yourself. Sit in the kitchen, eat her scones, win her over."

"You overestimate my charm, but I'll give it a go. Think she'll know anything useful?"

"Polly Treeve's been with the family thirty years," said Carol. "She'll know where the bodies are buried. Hell, she could have buried a few herself!"

Chapter Four

The route to Neville Bendix's house was quite straightforward, which made Carol think she'd probably been correct in thinking Larry Frobisher had intended to find some way to listen in to their interview with the pilot.

They followed in the plume of dust that billowed behind Frobisher's hulking four-wheel drive, halting behind him as he opened each long gate in the fencing. Every time, after they'd driven through, Carol leapt out and closed the gate after them. She grinned when Bourke remarked that Frobisher was making up for his insignificant size by surrounding himself with a massive vehicle, as she'd been thinking the same thing.

After about two kilometers, the windsock of the airfield came into view, and shortly they were drawing up in front of a small house situated beside a hangar. As they drove past it, Carol noticed it contained two planes.

With its red tiled roof, stone walls and white shutters, the neat cottage was a rather incongruous structure. It reminded Carol of an idealized English dwelling, surrounded by a verdant garden that was almost shockingly green when compared to the surrounding parched summer countryside.

"Can you find your own way back?" Frobisher called down from the lordly height of his outsized vehicle.

"No problem," said Bourke. "Thanks for your help."

Frobisher took off in a swirl of bad-tempered dust as Neville Bendix came to greet them. He was a short, stocky man with a heavily lined face and a luxuriant drooping mustache that looked glued on, although closer inspection persuaded Carol it was genuine.

Leading them into his kitchen, he said glumly, "I'm thinking I'm out of a job."

Bendix gestured for them to sit. One end of the kitchen table was covered with what looked like personal papers. Next to these was a chipped saucer full of butts, an open packet of cigarettes, a cheap lighter, and a can of Coke obviously not long from the fridge, as it was still beaded with condensation.

"Something to drink?" he asked.

"Water, please," said Carol, who was finding the heat trying. Bourke opted for a Coke.

The pilot got their drinks, then flung himself down in his chair. "How can I help you?"

"Tell us about Leapers Anonymous," said Bourke, settling himself with his notebook open on the table in front of him.

"Mr. Ryce was mad on skydiving. I was already his pilot when he formed this exclusive, invitation-only club and called it Leapers Anonymous. Anyone really into the sport knew about it, but not every person Mr. Ryce might accept as a possible member could afford the annual fees. Of course he was rich enough to pay for everything—he provided the plane and the airfield, for instance— but he often said to me that no one appreciated anything unless it cost them their own money, big time."

"Was Milton Ryce difficult to work for?" Carol asked.

Bendix took a swig from his Coke, wiped his mustache, and said, "I'd be the first to admit he could be pretty nasty to people, but he was always good to me. The kind of boss you do a little extra for, know what I mean? He trusted me to look after the care and maintenance of the aircraft. Didn't interfere, but expected the best. Paid me well, gave me this house rent free. It was a sweet deal, but I reckon now it's over. No way will Ted or Rae want to keep me on. Mrs. Ryce neither—she isn't into skydiving."

"I notice there are two aircraft in the hangar," Carol said.

"Mind if I smoke?" Without waiting for assent, he shook a Marlboro out of the pack and lit it. He sucked in a lungful of smoke, then exhaled it in a thin gray stream. "One of the aircraft is converted for skydiving, and that's all it's used for. The other is for passengers. I was on call twenty-four hours a day to fly Mr. Ryce—and guests, if he had any—wherever he wanted to go. Apart from business trips to different country centers, I mainly commuted between here and Sydney. Most Fridays I'd pick Mr. Ryce up at Bankstown airport and bring him back here for the weekend. Sunday evening or early Monday morning, I'd take him back to the city."

"You don't think his family will continue to fly up to Hash's Creek?" Carol asked.

Bendix shook his head. "Nah. They don't like the country that much. I reckon they'll sell this place as soon as they can put it on the market."

"Mr. Bendix, we'd like to hear about the flight yesterday morning," said Bourke. "Was there anything unusual about it?"

He took another quick pull at his cigarette, then balanced it carefully on the edge of the butt-filled saucer. "Nothing out of the ordinary . . . until Mr. Ryce . . ." His chin trembled.

"No arguments? Disagreements?"

Bendix cleared his throat. "Not a thing." He paused before saying, "Everything's been going round and round in my head, ever since." He looked directly into Carol's eyes. "Mr. Ryce—was it an accident, or deliberate? I want to know."

"We're not sure, Mr. Bendix."

"I heard on the grapevine that the APF guy said it was deliberate."

"The bush telegraph's been active."

Carol's dry comment got an acknowledging nod from Bendix. "You know how it is in the country. Everyone knows everyone else's business."

Carol decided that sharing information might make Bendix more likely to answer her questions freely, so she said, "The APF representative believes both the main and reserve chutes were tampered with, but we're getting a second opinion from Air Force experts."

"The APF bloke would know. I'd bank on what he said."

"Can you think of anyone who'd wish Mr. Ryce harm?"

Picking up his cigarette, Bendix examined the burning end of it for a moment, then said, "It's like Mr. Ryce went out of his way to make enemies. Know what I mean?"

"Do you have specific names?" Bourke asked.

Bendix looked up with a sour smile. "Wouldn't like to point the finger. Let's just say anyone who was a victim of one of his practical jokes. Add to that businesspeople who got the short end of the stick. That makes a long, long list."

He took several puffs from his cigarette, stubbed it out, and immediately lit a fresh one.

"I'd like to cover this weekend," said Carol. "Did you pick Mr. Ryce up in Sydney last Friday?"

"Not this time. He said he was driving."

"By himself?"

"I reckon Kym Watson would be with him, but I don't know for sure. Not my business."

"Did he often drive from Sydney to Hash's Creek? It's a good three hours."

"Sometimes, not often." He lifted a shoulder. "Dunno why he did this time. Going by air's a lot quicker. Anyway, he called me from Sydney on Friday and said that he had a party ready for a

Saturday morning jump, if the weather was okay. Didn't tell me who was in the party, and I didn't ask. Not my business."

"After this phone call, when was the next time you spoke to Mr. Ryce?"

"Saturday morning. I'd checked the weather forecast—it was ideal—and had everything ready to go. Ted and Mr. McNamara had already loaded everything when Mr. Ryce turned up with Kym. We all went through the details of the DZ—the drop zone—then Ted and Kym left for the landing site and we took off."

Interested that Bendix had referred to Kymberly Watson by her first name, when he referred to his employer and others more formally, Carol said, "You know Ms. Watson well?"

"Kym? She's a friendly sort. Doesn't stand on ceremony. Haven't known her long, but right from the start she insisted I call her Kym. I felt a bit uncomfortable at first, being so familiar in front of Mr. Ryce, but he laughed and said it was okay."

Bendix went on to give technical details of the flight, all of which Bourke dutifully copied down.

"So there were three passengers, plus you?"

"Yeah. Mr. Ryce, Ian McNamara and Verity Stuart. Mr. McNamara jumped first, then I went around and Mr. Ryce went out, then Ms. Stuart. It was a standard flight. There was nothing out of the ordinary."

"That morning, was anyone behaving differently?"

He scratched his nose. "Mr. McNamara was quiet, but that's his way. Ms. Stuart, she usually talks a bit—nerves, you know—but she hardly said a word. I remember thinking she and Mr. Ryce had had words. They often argued about things."

"Did Milton Ryce seem different in any way? Nervous? Worried?" Carol asked.

"I remember him being in a really good mood, grinning to himself and all. Thought he might be hatching some practical joke. I've noticed how he gets to looking pleased with himself when he's going to pull one off."

"You've seen him carry out practical jokes before?"

"Oh, yeah. I helped with the UFO hoax with that tennis player. And those alien crop circles out near Bathurst last year? I was one of the people tramping around flattening corn stalks in the middle of the night."

His tone was less than enthusiastic. Carol said, "Personally, what did you think of these practical jokes?"

He made a face. "Juvenile, really. Sort of thing you grow out of, but Mr. Ryce never did. Frankly, I didn't like getting involved in embarrassing people, but Mr. Ryce was picking up my paycheck, so I did what I was told."

Bourke flipped over pages in his notebook. "When we spoke to Ted Ryce, he said his father had intentionally tampered with Verity Stuart's main parachute so she'd continue to free-fall until she activated her reserve chute."

Bendix nodded slowly. "It's possible—sort of thing he'd do. It really annoyed Mr. Ryce that she would always pull the ripcord early. A few months ago he set up a mass jump with a couple of other clubs to have a go at breaking the Aussie record for the number of people simultaneously free-falling. Verity Stuart insisted on being part of it. Mr. Ryce said she ruined the attempt by panicking and opening her parachute too soon."

"So this would be to punish her?" said Carol.

"Something like that."

"How about Ian McNamara? Would he have known what was going on?"

"Doubt it. Mr. Ryce always said the fewer people were in on the practical joke, the better. Besides, if Mr. McNamara had known, he would have said something to stop her jumping. He'd already had words with Mr. Ryce about the gun he put in his luggage."

Bourke looked up from his notes. "What gun?"

"Last month Mr. McNamara was taking a business trip to New Zealand. Mr. Ryce arranged for the silhouette of a gun to be cut out of metal and hidden in Mr. McNamara's carry-on luggage. There was quite a scene at the airport when it showed up on the scanner, and Mr. McNamara missed his flight. He was absolutely furious about the whole thing."

"After that, why would McNamara have anything more to do with Ryce?" asked Bourke.

"I'd reckon it was a business decision. Ryce Industries is one of Ian McNamara's main clients. I'd say he couldn't run the risk of losing Mr. Ryce as a customer." He paused, almost about to say something more, then sat back, apparently deciding not to add anything.

Carol gave him a sympathetic smile. "This must be difficult for you, Mr. Bendix, but I must assure you how important it is for you to tell us everything you know."

"It's not something I'm sure of. It's something I heard. May not be true."

"About Ian McNamara?"

Bendix stared at Carol for a moment, his lips compressed, then he said, "Okay, I'll tell you. I heard that Mr. McNamara and Mr. Ryce's wife were . . . close. Very close."

"They were having an affair?"

He nodded reluctantly. "It may not be true."

"Who told you about this?"

"I don't want to say."

Bourke gave him an understanding smile. "I know what it's like, mate. You don't want people to think you blab everything you hear. Let's just say your name won't be mentioned. Okay?"

Another reluctant nod. "It was the chauffeur, Sandy Boyne. He plays his cards close to his chest. I was surprised when he told me." His lips twitched with the beginning of a smile. "But not half so surprised as Sandy was when Mrs. Ryce fired him."

"She fired him because of this gossip?"

He spread his hands. "Search me. But it's likely, isn't it? All I know for sure, though, is that Sandy was there one day and gone the next. I kept my mouth shut, didn't ask questions, but I figure Mrs. Ryce must have found out, and got rid of him."

"Did Milton Ryce mention anything about it?"

"No, but he wouldn't. He didn't discuss things with me. I was there to do a job, and I did it."

Carol asked a few more background questions, then mentioned the two parachute packs Ian McNamara had left in the hangar. They followed Bendix into the blast of furnace heat—late afternoon seemed as hot as midday had been—and over to the hangar, whose silver walls blindingly reflected the sun.

Inside, the welcome shade was only marginally cooler. A workbench was militarily neat. The two aircraft, obviously meticulously maintained, sat side-by-side. Seeing Carol looking at the one with LEAPERS ANONYMOUS! painted on the fuselage, Bendix said, "Sergeant Huffner's already been out to look her over, not that it meant anything to him, but he said it was an essential part of his investigation."

"We'll be sending someone, too. Just a formality," said Carol. "By the way, what's your take on Sergeant Huffner?"

Bendix looked wary. "What do you mean?"

"He told us Mr. Ryce had asked the sergeant to keep an eye on Rae Ryce. The implication was she was likely to get into trouble."

"Rae's a bit wild, but there's no real harm in her. I figure the worst she does is drive a bit too fast and maybe take recreational drugs at parties, just like pretty well everyone her age seems to do."

"And Sergeant Huffner turns a blind eye to this?"

"I don't blame Huffner. You've got to get on with people, especially ones with as much clout as Mr. Ryce." Clearly unhappy with the way the conversation was going, he added, "If there's nothing else, I'll get you the chutes."

Bourke indicated the two aircraft. "Are these the only planes that use the airfield?"

"Mostly. Sometimes one of Mr. Ryce's business associates will fly in on a company plane for a meeting."

They followed Bendix to the back of the hangar, where there was a separate concrete-floored room, as orderly and uncluttered as the hangar area. One wall held a series of wide cabinets, each labeled with a name. In the center were long benches. "If you're into doing it yourself, you pack your parachute right here."

"Is that what Mr. Ryce did this weekend?" Bourke asked.

"He was never one for doing things at the last moment, so I guess not. He always had his skydiving stuff ready to go well ahead of time."

"But it's here he would have tampered with Ms. Stuart's parachute?"

"I suppose so. Ms. Stuart wouldn't know how to pack a parachute herself. Maybe Mr. Ryce volunteered." He shrugged. "I dunno."

Opening two of the cabinets—one labeled *McNamara*, the other *Stuart*—he retrieved the two packs. He frowned at the roughly bundled orange parachutes, which clearly had been crammed in willy-nilly.

"What color was Mr. Ryce's parachute?" Carol asked.

"Same as these—orange. They've all got the Leapers Anonymous logo on them."

"So the chutes are interchangeable?"

"Everyone looked after their own equipment."

Examining the cabinets, Carol said, "There's no way to lock these?"

"No need. No one comes to the hangar but Leapers Anonymous members, me, the mechanic, and every six months or so, the APF guy to inspect the gear. As for any other staff, Mr. Ryce insists on stringent background checks."

Bourke, who'd been wandering around examining the room closely, indicated a door, half hidden by the bank of storage cabinets. "What's behind this?"

"Mr. Ryce's private office. Nothing to see, just a plain desk, a computer and filing cabinets. He kept anything to do with Leapers Anonymous there."

Bourke tried the door. "It's locked. Do you have a key?"

Bendix hesitated. "I'm not sure . . . Mr. Ryce being dead and all . . ."

Carol said crisply, "Mr. Ryce's death is shaping up to be a murder investigation, Mr. Bendix."

He looked at her for a moment, reluctance in every move, then fished in his pocket and brought out a large bunch of keys. Selecting one, he unlocked the door, switched on a light, then stood aside. "There's nothing of interest here."

It was a small room with no windows, so the only illumination was from artificial light. It contained, as Bendix had said, utilitarian office furniture: a metal desk bearing a flat-screen computer and two olive green filing cabinets. Rather incongruously, a brightly patterned rug lay on the concrete floor in front of the desk.

Carol looked at the rug, raised her eyebrows, then nodded to Bourke. He bent over, took one end of the rug, and flicked it out of the way. "What's this, Mr. Bendix?" he said.

Bendix looked stolidly down at the circular steel plate set into the floor. Carol thought he might be debating whether to play dumb, but after a moment he said, "It's a safe. Mr. Ryce had it installed when the hangar was built."

The heavy blue steel indicated the safe was an expensive model, opened by a combination lock. Bourke squatted down to check it was secure, then said, "Do you have the combination to open it?"

"No. Only Mr. Ryce had that."

"What's in it?" Carol asked, bending over to check the maker's name.

Bendix shrugged. "No idea." He tugged at one end of his mustache. "Nothing important. I reckon just papers to do with the Leapers."

Carol could sense his anxiety, and immediately wanted to see the contents. She'd need a court order to have the safe opened, and she didn't want to alert Bendix before that had been obtained. She strolled out of the room, saying, "I'm sure you're right, Mr. Bendix. I don't think we need worry about it."

A few minutes later, skydiving packs safely in the boot of the car, Carol waved a casual goodbye to Bendix. As she drove away from the pilot's cottage, she said, "Bendix knows more than he's saying."

"He's got a fair idea what's in the safe, I'd reckon."

"You noted the manufacturer and model?"

"I did. I'll check if the company has a regional office. If not, I guess we'll have to fly a locksmith up from Sydney."

"Let's get it open as fast as possible, Mark. We don't want anyone to get there before us."

"You don't think Bendix has the combination?"

"He wouldn't have shown so much tension if he knew whatever was in it was harmless—or if he'd already opened the safe and removed whatever was there."

"I'll get on to it," said Bourke. "I'm developing a burning desire to know what's in it, myself."

Soon they were at the last gate before Ryce Hall. "How about chatting up the locals this evening?" Bourke said, wiping his face as he got back into the car. "I could do with a beer, I can tell you!"

"Everyone will know we're the cops from the city. That might discourage heart-to-hearts."

Bourke grinned at her. "Ryce and his entourage are from the Big Smoke, too. I'll lay you odds the citizens of Hash's Creek will be delighted to dish the dirt, and by now everyone and his dog will know Ryce was likely murdered."

Carol drove past Ryce Hall without stopping, although Frobisher was in the front and waved to them. "I want an in-depth check on that gentleman," said Carol, returning Frobisher's salutation. "There's something about him that doesn't quite ring true."

"He's a leech," said Bourke, disdain in his voice. "And a poisonous one, at that."

Chapter Five

Bourke was almost immediately proved correct about the locals being willing to gossip. As soon as they had stopped the car in the parking area at the rear of the Hash's Creek Hotel, the proprietor, a tall, hard-faced woman with dyed red hair and a clarion voice, appeared at the back entrance. "Inspector Ashton, Sergeant Bourke—there's been a call. I took the liberty of jotting down a message for you."

Carol took the note and glanced at it quickly. Sergeant Huffner had called with important—this word was underlined twice—information. "Thank you, Ms. Sandys."

"Joycie, call me Joycie!"

"Thank you, Joycie."

Leading the way inside to the comparative coolness of the dimly lit hallway, Joycie said, "I'm wondering if you'll be having dinner in the dining room this evening."

Not waiting for a reply, she strode along the hall and into the reception area at the front of the building. There she paused, showing disconcertingly grayish teeth in an inviting smile. "If so, you're more than welcome to join our local citizens for an after-dinner drink in the bar. On the house, of course, seeing as you're visitors up from the city."

"We'll be in for dinner," said Bourke with an amused glance at Carol. "And I'm sure the Inspector and I would be delighted to join everyone later for a drink."

"Not on the house, however," said Carol. "We're on official business, as I'm sure you're aware."

Joycie's long face became instantly solemn. "Tragic, tragic," she said, "Miltie Ryce dying that way."

"Miltie?" said Bourke. "I've never heard his name shortened from Milton."

"That's what we call him behind his back. He's a bit lord-of-the-manorish, know what I mean? Just our little joke to take him down a peg or two." Her expression grew even more grave. "But no one would wish that upon him. Falling out of the sky. Dreadful business."

"Mr. Ryce wasn't popular in these parts?" Carol inquired.

Joycie blew out her cheeks. "The things I could tell you! But of course, I mustn't. That'd be gossip."

Carol saw Bourke's lips twitch. She was close to smiling herself. "Joycie," she said, "may I be perfectly frank?"

Joycie clasped her hands to her breast. "Oh, please, Inspector, *do* be frank, by all means."

"Conveying information to the police is not gossip. We're very grateful for anything that might assist with our inquiries."

Given this reassurance, Joycie beamed. "Come into the office. We can speak privately there."

She took them into a pokey little room half filled by an antique rolltop desk. "Dad's," she said, indicating it with a gesture. "Didn't have the heart to get rid of it once he passed on. All I have of him, really, apart the pub."

She directed Carol to a spindly chair, bustled outside and came back with a stool for Bourke, then seated herself in an old office chair that from its battered yet graceful frame seemed to belong to the same era as the desk.

"What can you tell us?" said Carol, priming the pump.

There was no need: Joycie was overflowing with information. After a discourse on how Milton Ryce had bought the old Carlisle property, demolished the perfectly sound, historical farmhouse, and built a totally unnecessary new structure, she launched into the noise pollution caused by constant flights.

"We may not have our own aerodrome, but we're not backward here in Hash's Creek," she declared. "However, this constant sky-diving and noisy little planes flying everywhere is too much. Frightens cattle, disturbs the peace. I blame the local council members. When Dad was mayor it never would have happened. They shouldn't have agreed to allow Miltie Ryce to build an air-field. And when they did cave in, they should have had the back-bone to impose restrictions. As it is now, planes can fly in at all times of day and night."

"Really?" said Bourke. "We got the impression there were only occasional flights."

"Who told you that?"

"Mr. Ryce's pilot, Neville Bendix."

"Oh, *Nev*," said Joycie with scorn. "Pathetic little puppet, mouthing the Miltie line. I mean, I applaud loyalty, who doesn't? But Nev Bendix takes it to extremes. He'd defend the devil, if the devil was called Miltie Ryce!"

Once upstairs in her basically furnished but comfortable room, Carol used her mobile phone to return Huffner's call. She avoided using the room phone, having a suspicion Joycie was quite capable of monitoring the conversation.

"I've been asking around, and I've located Kymberly Watson," Huffner announced triumphantly. "I know you've been out at Ryce Hall, but when you saw Rae and Ted, I guarantee they didn't let on she was there under wraps." He paused, perhaps expecting Carol to say something to indicate her surprise, then went on, "That's where Kymberly Watson is. Ryce Hall."

"We've already spoken with Ms. Watson. Mr. Frobisher told us she was there."

"Oh," said Huffner, completely deflated. "I'd have been happy to cover that interview for you."

"Thank you for the offer, Sergeant. There is a matter you might help me with. Rae Ryce didn't return to the Hall as she indicated to us she would. Do you have some idea where she might be?"

"Most likely Rae's gone back to Sydney. She doesn't work, you know, so she doesn't have to worry about a job. She just does whatever she pleases."

There was such a note of censure in his voice that Carol said, "You don't approve?"

After a moment's pause, he said, "That's not for me to say." He cleared his throat. "Now, Inspector, you ask where she might be. If Rae's still around here, she could be at the Clements' place. She often stays there. Want me to check?"

"That won't be necessary, Sergeant. I'm about to call the Clements to set up an interview."

"I'm wondering," said Huffner, "how long you're intending to stay in Hash's Creek. It seems to me most of the witnesses have gone back to Sydney."

Carol grinned to herself. It was plain Huffner resented city cops tramping around his patch and was keen to get rid of them as soon as possible.

"I'll be returning to the city tomorrow," she said.

"Good, good." Then, apparently realizing this might be construed the wrong way, Huffner hastened to add, "I mean I can hold the fort here."

"Detective Sergeant Bourke will be staying in Hash's Creek to tie up some loose ends."

"Loose ends?"

"We'll need a court order to search Milton Ryce's property," Carol said. "Can you line up a local judge tomorrow?"

"Looking for something in particular?"

Not wanting her interest in Milton Ryce's safe to become common knowledge before it was opened, she said, "The search warrant's more a procedural matter than anything else."

Sergeant Huffner, obviously not pleased that Bourke was remaining in Hash's Creek, rang off, assuring Carol he would contact a magistrate about a search warrant.

Carol picked up the hotel's phone and was rewarded with Joycie's eager, "Can I help you, Inspector?"

"Would you know Basil and Morris Clements' phone number, by any chance?"

"Of course! I'll get it for you."

After a brief conversation with Basil Clement to set up an appointment for early the next morning, Carol said, "By the way, Mr. Clement, I was wondering whether Rae Ryce happens to be staying with you."

"Rae? No, sorry. Like to help you out, but haven't seen hide nor hair of her. She's got lots of friends. Could be anywhere. Gone back to Sydney, for instance."

Carol put down the phone thoughtfully. Basil Clement hadn't needed to say that much. A simple no would have sufficed. In her experience, liars often over-explained.

She was preparing to have a quick shower, when her mobile phone trilled. "Carol," said her Aunt Sarah, "you're going to throw me a party."

"I am?"

"Yes, you are, darling. Don't sound so negative. I'm your sole and only aunt, remember?"

"How could I forget?"

Aunt Sarah ignored Carol's sardonic tone. "I have a birthday coming up—you know that. But now there's another thing to celebrate."

Carol often had a sinking feeling when speaking with Aunt Sarah. She had one now. "What is it?"

"Darling, I know you'll be thrilled for me. I've just been elected president of Eco-Crones for the Environment. There were several vying for the honor, but in the end, I won. Bit of a landslide, really."

"Congratulations."

"And Carol, this has happened just at the point when the Eco-Crones are going international! Your aunt will be president of a worldwide ecological movement of older women dedicated to saving the planet. Imagine that!"

"I'm imagining, with some trepidation," said Carol. "This doesn't mean by any chance you will travel to strange and exotic places, does it?"

"Absolutely! As well as the States and Europe. And China, of course. China and Russia—both ecological hell, you know."

Carol pictured her headstrong aunt staging one of her flamboyant demonstrations and ending up in a Chinese jail. She had no doubt Aunt Sarah would regard such incarceration as a badge of honor. "I have some misgivings—"

"Carol! You really must think more positively. What could be more important than combating global warming? Saving the lungs of Shanghai babies? Not to mention the perilous state of the world's oceans. And indiscriminate use of pesticides! Golf courses, for example."

Aware that Aunt Sarah had a somewhat irrational loathing of golf courses, Carol hastened to get her off the subject. "Is this party to be at my place, or yours?"

"Yours, darling, if you don't mind. My house in the Blue Mountains just isn't big enough. And you do have those lovely wide decks. It'll be perfect."

Fearing the answer, Carol said, "Just how many are you thinking of inviting?"

"Quite a few . . ."

"Twenty? Forty? Give me some idea."

"The Eco-Crones have a promotional budget, quite a substantial one. I'm sure the treasurer and board will authorize a generous amount. After all, it'll be excellent publicity for the organization."

"Oh, *Aunt*," said Carol. "How many?"

"Could be a hundred. Maybe more. And the media, of course."

"Aunt Sarah, something this size would be better at a function center, don't you think?"

Her aunt ignored this hopeful question. "It occurs to me, darling, parking's going to be a problem, with all those narrow streets around your place. Fortunately, you, being a police officer, should be able to look after that area . . ."

Over dinner in the pub's dining room Bourke chuckled as Carol recounted her conversation. "Aunt Sarah," he said, shaking his head. "What a woman! You wouldn't catch me standing in her way. She'd mow me down."

"I tried to persuade her to hire some function place where all the details would be looked after by professionals. But no. She's insisting she wants a homey atmosphere. *Homey*, with hordes of strangers descending on the quiet suburb of Seaforth. The mind boggles."

Carol's beautiful house, overhung by eucalyptus gums, overlooked the sleepy blue-green reaches of Middle Harbour. It sat at the top of a cliff, above a precipitous fall to the deep water below. Originally Carol's parents' home, it had been extensively remodeled. It was a delightful place to live: The wide wooden decks caught cooling breezes in summer, and the gardens, containing only indigenous plants, attracted butterflies, birds, and native animals. Even the presence of Sinker, Carol's black-and-white cat, failed to discourage the possums or deter the huge blue-tongue lizard who'd set up residence in a rocky corner of the yard.

"Once she realizes how much work it is, maybe Aunt Sarah will change her mind and agree to a different venue," said Bourke.

"Have you ever known my aunt to change her mind?"

Bourke laughed. "Well, no," he admitted.

"I'm doomed," said Carol.

As befitting the National Trust status of Hash's Creek Hotel, the bar had been restored to its original Spartan form, although the historical exclusion of women from this drinking area—barmaids excepted—was no longer observed.

The walls were vertical planks stained dark brown. Vintage posters touting old-time alcoholic beverages provided the only concession to decoration. The high ceiling was whitewashed. The floor would have originally been spread with sawdust to soak up beer spills, but now was bare wooden boards. There was nowhere to sit, so patrons collected their orders, then moved away from the bar to stand in groups, holding their drinks.

There was a long, wide bar, complete with brass railing running the whole length, a few inches above the floor. This railing was for the comfort of the customer, who would rest one foot upon it while attempting to catch a barmaid's attention.

Behind the bar, bottles with labels of many colors were arranged on shelves. The cloudy mirror reflected back distorted images, proof of its handcrafted era. The handles of the draft beer pumps were white porcelain inlaid with metal scrolling. An antiquated cash register, though not in use, sat in archaic beauty, displaying its high-set brass keys and gleaming ebony sides.

Even though it was Sunday night, the bar was crowded. The noise of half-shouted conversations and guffawing laughter ricocheted off the walls in a convivial din.

"Perhaps you'd prefer the Ladies' Lounge," Joycie half-shouted to be heard. "You can sit at a table and it's much quieter."

The noise level appreciably dropped as she said these last words, so her voice boomed out, much too loud. The collective eyes of the patrons took in Carol and Bourke, both of whom were dressed casually in jeans. After a pause, there was a renewed buzz of conversation.

"Here in the bar will be fine," Carol said.

Joycie, obviously approving, beamed at her. "I'll leave you to your own devices, then." She looked around, then added with satisfaction, "Big crowd tonight. I'm needed behind the counter."

Plowing through the crowd in that direction, Joycie stopped here and there to greet patrons. While speaking with a tall, olive-skinned man, she gestured toward Carol. The man nodded, his expression full of quizzical interest.

Carol and Bourke had agreed to work the room separately. "You're on your own, Mark," she said to him. "Just don't get into a stoush with the locals."

"You know I'm not a fighter," said Bourke virtuously, "so if anyone starts something, I'll have to call on you for help."

Carol smiled at this. Mark Bourke was tall, broad shouldered and very fit. He didn't take a punishing daily run like Carol, but he worked out regularly. Carol couldn't think of anyone she'd rather have beside her if physical violence threatened.

While he headed toward a large clump of middle-aged men nursing their beers, Carol made her way to the bar. After squeezing between two patrons, she rested her elbows on the edge of the bar, put her right foot on the brass railing in the time-honored manner, and assessed her companions.

The man on her left, pot-bellied and balding, was gazing morosely into his drink. He grunted something inaudible when she said hello, and ostentatiously turned his back to her. The woman on her right, concentrated on juggling three full-to-the-brim glasses of beer, moved away to deliver her bounty to waiting friends. She was replaced by a young woman whose small, pinched features were set in a determined scowl. She had her mousy hair scraped back into a tight ponytail. "Inspector Ashton?"

Carol nodded agreeably. "That's me."

The young woman fished around in her shoulder bag and came up with a notebook and pen. "I'm Yvonne Knight, reporter for the *Messenger*."

"A journalist?"

Yvonne looked pleased to be given this title. "It's the largest regional paper in this area, Inspector. I'm hoping you'll make a statement about your investigation of Milton Ryce's tragic death."

"No statement."

"What about a photo? I've got a camera in my car."

Carol smiled at the reporter's persistence. "No photo."

"I've heard that it wasn't an accident. Would you care to comment?"

"I'm afraid not."

Yvonne's shoulders slumped. "Bummer," she said. "My editor will kill me. He says I have to be tenacious. Never take no for an answer." She gave Carol a beseeching look. "This is my first big story."

"I presume you live in the area," said Carol, amused by Yvonne's plaintive expression.

"Born and bred in Hash's Creek," said Yvonne. "And believe me, I don't intend to spend my whole life here. First I have to make my name as a journalist, then I'm aiming to get a job at a big city paper."

"Maybe we can make a trade," said Carol. "You can take a photo of me and Sergeant Bourke tomorrow morning when we're both more suitably dressed. In return, I'd like some background information on the town and the people in it."

Yvonne's face was bright with enthusiasm. "It's a deal!"

"Just one question before you go. I keep hearing about illegal drugs in Hash's Creek. What's available?"

"Marijuana. That's a given—most grown locally. Quite a lot of ecstasy, especially at parties. The kids are really into that."

Carol hid her smile. Yvonne wasn't much more than a kid herself. "Hard stuff?" she asked.

"Didn't much used to be, but since Mr. Ryce and city people like him started coming, there's certainly more around. Some cocaine, but not much heroin. Lots more meth lately, though."

Carol was very aware the production of methamphetamine held the promise of great financial gain to criminals. Whereas it took three months to grow a large marijuana crop, a million dollars' worth of meth could be concocted in a garage over one weekend. And marijuana crops were difficult to conceal—meth labs could be set up in trailers and taken from place to place.

"Local labs making it?" she asked.

Yvonne, clearly chagrined not to have the information, said, "Inspector, I don't know. Wish I did." Her face lit up. "This could be a *big* story. Maybe one that'll get me noticed by a city newspaper."

"Hold on," said Carol, concerned that the young reporter would blithely put herself in harm's way. "Anyone involved in meth production or distribution is dangerous, Yvonne. Very dangerous. I'll put you in touch with someone in the state crime drug squad for background information. She'll make it clear how hazardous it is to go chasing after these crims."

After extracting a pledge that Yvonne would not pursue the story before being thoroughly briefed, Carol arranged to meet her after breakfast the next day, and Yvonne left to canvass for local responses to Ryce's death.

"You're the Sydney cop," said a deep baritone voice. It was the man to whom Joycie had been speaking earlier. He was younger than she'd first thought and quite handsome, with smooth olive skin, dark eyes and thick black hair.

"I'm one of two Sydney cops," she said.

"Ah, but you're the inspector. The one with the power." His smile revealed a distinct gap between his upper front teeth. Carol vaguely remembered reading somewhere this was supposed to indicate good humor.

A frothing glass of beer was abruptly slapped down in front of Carol. "On the house!" exclaimed Joycie from the other side of the bar. "Don't argue."

"How about me, Joycie?" said the gap-toothed man with a fetching smile. "Don't I deserve one on the house, too?"

"Mind your manners, Stevie, or I'll get Frankie here to toss you out." She jerked her head toward a bulky, bullet-headed man, pulling beers.

Carol, quietly amused at the surfeit of names ending with "ie," said, "Let me buy you a drink, Stevie, since I apparently am not allowed to pay for my own."

"Hey," he said. "Cool."

Joycie snorted, but the glass of amber fluid arrived in front of Stevie almost immediately. Joycie winked at Carol as she took her money. "No need to pay to loosen Stevie's tongue. He's capable of talking the legs off an iron pot."

Stevie's Adam's apple rippled as he took a long swallow of his beer. He smacked his lips. "What do you want to know, Inspector? Who cut the lines on Miltie's parachute?"

"You have someone in mind?"

"Several. But not doing your job. You'll have to narrow it down to one suspect, yourself." He looked around conspiratorially.

No one seemed to be paying them any attention. "I think it might be safe to speak," said Carol in a dry tone.

Stevie grinned. "Just checking who's here. Last thing I want is a slander suit slapped on me."

"Slander? This is a private conversation."

Stevie snorted. "You tell Dr. Gilbert bloody Edmundson that. He overheard me chatting with my mates about Rae, and he threatened to have me in court. Said the cops were in his pocket, so I'd be arrested, no trouble. Then he'd bring the lawyers in and take me for every cent I've got." He paused to let this sink in, then added, "I was dead set to deck him, but my mates stopped me."

"Wise move," said Carol. "You don't want to be looking at an assault charge."

"And Rae wouldn't even talk to me after that."

"This would be Rae Ryce?"

"Yeah. She's a wild one."

"How do you know her?"

"Every time her Dad makes Rae come up here, she says she nearly dies of boredom. Goes looking for trouble, and a pub's a good place to start. I ran into her one night last year, and one thing led to another."

"Drugs?"

It was obvious Stevie had suddenly remembered Carol was a cop, as a look of consternation appeared on his face. "Hey, let's get this straight. Not *me*. I don't do drugs."

Chapter Six

Much later that evening, Carol and Bourke sat in the deserted Ladies' Lounge to compare notes. Joycie had bustled in with a large pot of coffee and slices of cinnamon cake—"In case you feel a bit peckish"—and then left them alone.

"What did you pick up?" Carol asked.

"Mostly the sort of things you'd expect. Ryce was good for Hash's Creek. Ryce was bad for Hash's Creek. Apparently he single-handedly started a boom in property prices. After Ryce built the Hall, several other entrepreneurial types decided they wanted a country retreat, too."

"Including the Clement brothers."

"The Clement brothers are not highly regarded," said Bourke, waving a admonishing finger. "Particularly Basil. His infamy preceded him, so none of the locals seemed surprised at reports of disgraceful goings on at his place in the hills. In fact, they seemed to quite enjoy telling me about dissolute parties, vehicles driving through fences, drunken brawls, naked bathing in Hash's Creek . . ."

It was the Clement brothers who were supposed to lunch with Ryce and Kymberly Watson on Saturday. Basil Clement had been a world class golfer, among the top international money winners, until his taste for continuous, hard partying affected his game. After a catastrophic drop in the rankings, Basil had abandoned golf and embraced a hedonistic lifestyle that kept both his name and various scandalous pictures of his exploits in the gossip magazines.

Basil's older and much quieter sibling Morris had acted as his business manager on the tour, accompanying him to every golf tournament. After Basil's retirement from the sport, Morris remained close to his brother. In photographs, Morris was frequently a peripheral figure, while Basil mugged for the camera center stage.

"I also picked up several references to illegal drugs," said Bourke, "but it was all to do with those wicked big-city types, including the Clements. Apparently the clean-living citizens of Hash's Creek don't take anything harder than an aspirin."

"Did Rae Ryce come up?"

"Several times, but not with the dislike her father's name elicited. A couple of worthy citizens felt sorry for her. One remarked it wasn't surprising Rae was a handful, since she had Milton Ryce for a parent."

"Was Ryce mentioned in reference to drugs?"

Bourke shook his head. "Not at all. The general consensus was that Milton Ryce had no idea what a fast crowd his daughter was running with."

"How about the son, Ted?" Carol asked. "I couldn't find anyone to say anything complimentary about him."

"I'm not surprised, after the practical joke Ted played on the town's mayor. Nobody but Ted was amused by that."

"It was *outrageous!*" Joycie, fresh coffee pot in hand, had entered the room and obviously overheard Bourke's comment.

She came over to their table, deftly switched the new coffee pot for the old, and stood back to say emphatically, "God knows, I've got very little time for Edith Costello. In my opinion, as a mayor,

61

she's a disaster. Nevertheless, there was no call for the Ryce boy to set her up that way."

"Were you there when it happened?"

"I was, Inspector. An eyewitness." Her garish hair seemed to glow redder with indignation. "Absolute disgrace! Would you like an accurate account?"

"Please," said Carol.

Joycie put down the coffee pot she was holding to leave her hands free to gesticulate. "Of course, it was all an act," she said, "but at the time, it looked very genuine. Ted Ryce"—she spat out his name—"got a couple of his city friends to play a young married couple, pushing their baby along Main Street in a stroller. Another friend lured Edith out of the mayor's office on some pretext. I don't know if you've noticed, but there's a pedestrian crossing right in front of the Town Hall."

"We've noticed," said Bourke obligingly.

"Well! You suddenly hear the baby in the stroller crying hard, but the couple pays no attention and starts across the road in the pedestrian crossing. Suddenly, out of nowhere, a car roars into view, hits the stroller and sends the baby rocketing into the air, still wailing!"

Joycie paused for Carol and Bourke to visualize this horrifying moment, then continued, "The car keeps going, the baby hits the surface of the road with an awful thud. Silence, no more crying. The couple just stand there on the crossing. Edith, who's right there when it happens, shrieks, 'The baby! The baby!' and literally runs around in circles, flapping her arms. She really is a *stupid* woman."

"And then?" prompted Carol.

"All the traffic stops. Everyone around is staring, shocked. The couple walk over to the little bundle lying near the mangled stroller. They bend over to inspect the body. Edith, still twittering, has pulled herself together enough to join them. The couple straighten up, and the woman says to Edith, 'The baby's a goner, unfortunately. Bad luck, eh?' Edith just looks at her, mouth gaping. 'But it's your *baby*,' Edith shrieks. The mother shrugs. The man takes the young woman's arm. 'Oh, well,' he says, 'it's tiresome, but we'll just have to have another one.' With that, Edith loses it completely and starts screaming that it's their *baby*, don't they care?"

"What were you doing while all this was going on?" Carol inquired.

"Me?" said Joycie. "I was on my mobile phone, calling for help. Doing what Edith should have done, if she wasn't such an idiot. Of course, I didn't know the baby was a life-size doll wired to cry like a real child, so the moment the accident happened I put a call through to the ambulance and then the cops. Sergeant Huffner arrived just as that ghastly Ryce boy got out of the parked car where he was hidden, filming everything. The bastard got a perfect closeup of Edith's face just at the moment she realized she was the victim of a practical joke and had made a total exhibition of herself."

"But everyone else was fooled, too," said Bourke. "Even you, Joycie."

"Not one of us carried on like Edith Costello. And what about upholding the dignity of the office she holds? Complete failure there. Worse, when Ted Ryce had the film shown on local television for everyone to snigger at, Edith did nothing. Too embarrassed. Me? I'd have sued the pants off the little swine." Joycie added in a tone of quiet satisfaction, "Edith won't be mayor of this town again."

"Were any charges filed over the incident?" Carol asked.

Joycie's expression grew grim. "There *should* have been charges—disturbing the peace at the very least, I would have thought. But Sergeant Huffner was talked out of it." She added darkly, "You might like to investigate that, Inspector Ashton. Smells like police corruption to me."

"Thank you for giving us such a detailed account," said Carol. "We'll follow it up."

Carol thought Sergeant Huffner was going to have a lot more than this relatively minor dereliction of duty to worry about, but she made a mental note to add it to her report.

Joycie surveyed their table. "You've fresh coffee, but would you prefer tea? How about a toasted cheese sandwich?"

Carol saw the longing look on Bourke's face. His wife, Pat, frowned at what she called junk food, so he had a conspicuously healthy diet at home. It was a standing joke at work that any criminal who thought of bribing Bourke could dispense with money— a hamburger would do it.

"Sergeant Bourke would be very pleased with a toasted cheese sandwich," said Carol, "but nothing for me, thanks."

"With potato chips, Sergeant?"

Carol grinned when Bourke hesitated, obviously torn. "That's a yes," she said to Joycie. "He'd like the works."

Carol went up to bed exhausted. It had been a long day, starting very early this morning when Bourke had picked her up at Seaforth to begin the drive to Hash's Creek. The forecast for the coastal regions had promised fine, warm weather, and Carol had been looking forward to a lazy Sunday in the garden. Milton Ryce's precipitate fall into a country paddock had finished that idea. The moderate warmth of a Sydney day had been replaced by much more fiery inland temperatures.

Fatigued though she was, Carol couldn't get to sleep. She considered the logistics of Aunt Sarah's party and groaned. Resolutely pushing such thoughts out of her head, she tried counting backwards from a hundred. Then five hundred. The bed wasn't particularly comfortable, and she'd changed position for the umpteenth time. Just when she decided she'd be awake all night, she fell asleep.

Perhaps it was because Aunt Sarah had mentioned the wide decks on Carol's house, in her dream she was there, at her home. It wasn't as it looked now, but earlier, before she'd gutted the structure and rebuilt.

It was a quiet, sunny morning. Carol stood outside her front door. Puzzled, she looked down at the gun in her hand. She could hear bees buzzing in the flowers, a flash of blue—a little wren building a nest in a garden shrub.

Something dreadful was in the house.

Carol saw herself step forward through the door. "Come in," said an amused male voice. "You're in time to see Sybil die. And it's your fault. Your fault."

In the way of dreams, time and space were elastic. Abruptly Carol was in her sitting room. As if looking through the wrong end of a telescope, she saw Sybil's body slumped on a brightly colored mat. Her wrists were handcuffed. Her ashen face made her hair seem very red. Her mouth and jaw were bruised and swollen.

"Sybil's dying," remarked the male voice. "She fought me hard, but I suffocated her until she gasped for air. Then I poured it down her throat."

The dream Carol didn't need to ask what Sybil had been forced to drink—she knew. It was the hallucinogenic party drug GHB, fatal in large doses. An overwhelming despair gripped Carol. The drug was destroying Sybil, cell by cell, while nightmare images danced behind her closed eyes.

"Why?" asked Carol, turning to see her smiling tormentor. She knew his face, knew who he was, but couldn't remember his name. "Why Sybil?"

"Because of you. You made me do it. It's all your fault."

With teeth-gritting effort, Carol raised the gun she held. Heavy as lead, it swayed in her hand.

"You can't kill me," he said, laughing, his teeth growing in his mouth like tombstones, larger and larger. Carol fired again and again, the gun jumping in her hand like a live thing. The teeth shattered into piles of rubble. The laughter stopped.

Then slowly, slowly, dread closing her throat, Carol dared to look at Sybil. She lay as before, unmoving, unconscious. Then with shocking suddenness, her eyes opened, and she was staring up at Carol. Bright blood gushed from her chest, her mouth, her nose.

"Look what you've done to me, Carol," she said. "You've killed me."

Carol started awake, Sybil's accusing words ringing in her ears. She sat up in the darkness, groped for the bedside lamp, blinked in the glare as the prosaic realities of the hotel room sprang into comforting life.

Her nightmare had been a version of reality. It hadn't quite happened that way, although in a sense it *had* been Carol's fault. She'd overlooked something that indicated Sybil could be in danger, and she would always feel a measure of guilt for her oversight.

On that horrifying day, Sybil had been almost fatally drugged. She hadn't been shot, hadn't died . . . but their relationship, only just renewed, had sustained a slowly bleeding, fatal wound.

Since that defining event, Carol and Sybil had come together, then parted, several times. Eventually they'd both gone on to other relationships.

Carol had to acknowledge with uncharacteristic introspection that the defining issue between them was Carol's refusal to give up her home. Traumatized by the attack, Sybil had said she could never return to live in Carol's house. To move had been unthinkable, so Carol had said, "I'll totally change it," and she had, remodeling and extending the building until the room where Sybil had been tortured no longer existed in recognizable form.

This compromise had failed. Therapy hadn't enabled Sybil to overcome her abhorrence. The possibility of losing Sybil hadn't been enough to change Carol's decision to stay in her beloved home.

The final wisps of nightmare dissolved. Carol turned off the light and lay down again. Putting her arms behind her head, she stared into the darkness. Why was that building in Seaforth so important to her? In the past, she'd refused to move for Sybil. Now, in the present, her house had figured in her decision to reject the idea of joining Leota in the United States.

Carol knew she'd rationalized the two determining factors keeping her in Australia—her son and her job. Now she acknowledged to herself the house, too, was an anchor she might never cast off.

Chapter Seven

On Monday morning Carol and Bourke ate breakfast in the hotel dining room, which was furnished in a utilitarian manner with coir matting covering the floor, and commonplace chairs and tables. Other guests glanced at them with curiosity, but no one other than a self-effacing waiter came near their table until Joycie sailed through the door.

She was immediately the focus of everyone's attention, calling out in her stentorian voice, "Inspector! I'd advise you not to go out the front entrance. The TV people are there, and God knows who else. I've forbidden them to enter the premises, so they're lying in wait for you outside."

Bourke said to Carol, "I'd say one word has brought the media back with a vengeance, and that word is murder."

Joycie beckoned urgently to someone out in the hallway. "Come on, Yvonne. Don't be shy." Turning to Carol and Bourke, she went on, "Known Yvonne since she was a kid. She tells me she's got an exclusive with you, so I let her in."

All eyes were on Yvonne Knight as she attempted a casual entry. The effect was rather spoiled when she managed to trip on the coir matting and drop her notebook.

"Sorry," she said, her face red. "I asked Joycie if I could join you. It'd be hopeless trying to catch you outside."

Bourke rose and gallantly pulled out a chair. "Have coffee with us. Or tea, if you'd rather."

Yvonne slid onto the seat. Placing her camera and notebook on the table, she said, "Have you seen the telly this morning? Wasn't it *gross*, watching Mr. Ryce hit the ground like that? This story's really going to put Hash's Creek on the map. My editor's already been speaking to one of the city papers." She looked hopefully at Carol. "I'll get a Sydney byline if I come up with something good."

"I haven't watched television this morning," said Carol. "What exactly did you see?"

"They showed it in slow motion, which made it much worse . . . Mr. Ryce falling out of the sky and crashing into the ground."

Carol had safely dispatched the camcorder and DVD by courier to Sydney for analysis. It was clear a copy of Ryce's fatal plunge had been made before the camcorder had been given to her. Quietly furious, she said, "Was the source of this footage mentioned?"

Yvonne shook her head. "But I know where it came from."

"Larry Frobisher," said Bourke.

"Wrong," said Yvonne smugly. "It was Ted Ryce. It's supposed to be confidential, but I heard he sold it to a TV network for megabucks."

"I'd have bet on Frobisher doing something slimy like cashing in on someone's death, but to have Ted Ryce do it to his own father . . ." Bourke shook his head.

"And he did have the gall to lecture us on the possibility a cop might sneak it to the media," said Carol.

"Like father, like son," said Bourke. "I've a strong feeling

Milton Ryce would've approved. In the same circumstances, I reckon he'd have done likewise."

They were sitting in their car, having posed for the photograph for Yvonne. Now they were waiting for Joycie to unlock a gate at the rear of the hotel parking area. When she gesticulated, Bourke dutifully pulled up beside her, putting down the window when she tapped on it.

"Right," she hissed, as though the media gathered at the front of the hotel might overhear, "go down that laneway until you come to a T intersection. Turn left. That'll take you to Main Street. Okay?"

"Thank you, Joycie."

"You've got my directions of how to get to Basil Clement's place?"

"Thank you again, Joycie."

She slapped the side of the car. "Go!"

"That Joycie's a hoot," said Bourke, as they followed directions.

"I think she fancies you," said Carol with a grin as they turned onto Main Street.

The nearest commercial airport to Hash's Creek was fifty kilometers away. Carol was booked to fly back to Sydney, leaving Bourke the car for transportation as he followed up leads and checked out stories.

Her flight was at one o'clock, so there was time to interview the Clement brothers before she left. Bourke stifled a yawn as he drove down Hash's Creek's main thoroughfare, which was showing considerably more activity than when they'd arrived the day before.

"How did you sleep?" he asked. "I had way too much coffee, and my eyes kept popping open."

"I slept," said Carol, "but it was hardly restful." For a moment she was almost tempted to tell Bourke about her nightmare. Instead she said lightly, "Could be because I have a suspicion Aunt Sarah is adding multiple names to her guest list for the party."

"I think it very likely."

"Thank you, Mark. I needed that reassurance."

He gave her an affectionate smile. "How long have we worked together?"

"Don't ask."

She thought of the years they'd been colleagues, and the many cases they'd solved. With concern that everything might change between them, she said, "It's not absolutely definite my promotion to chief inspector will go through, you know."

"It's in the bag. Should have happened long ago."

"You're one to talk."

"Pat's been on about my lack of ambition," he said with a rueful grin. "I said I was quite content. She said I wasn't. For peace in the household, naturally I had to agree with her."

"Oh, sure," said Carol. "Poor little henpecked you."

On the surface, Mark Bourke and Pat James didn't seem an ideal pair, with Pat deeply into the art world and Bourke a more than conscientious detective, but their marriage was one of the strongest Carol knew. She was fond of Pat, whose ebullient, can-do take on life was infectious.

They chatted about Mark Bourke's pride and joy, his little girl, then moved on to the case at hand. The company that manufactured the safe did have a large regional presence, and a specialist locksmith would be in Hash's Creek that afternoon.

All the parachute packs used on the ill-fated jump on Saturday had been dispatched to Air Force experts. Carol had no doubt there would be confirmation of the Australian Parachute Federation's finding that Milton Ryce's gear had been tampered with. She was also sure Ted Ryce's story that his father had disabled Verity Stuart's main parachute would prove to be accurate.

"Mark, follow up on the air traffic into Ryce's private airfield. Joycie claims it was heavy, but Bendix gave us the impression there were only occasional visitors. I'll get Anne to run a check on flight plans filed for the last six months."

"Okay, Carol. I'll ask around, and also follow up on Rae Ryce's social activities."

"And Sergeant Huffner," said Carol. "I think he deserves a second look."

"He seemed to enjoy himself on the news this morning," Bourke remarked.

Before they'd left the hotel and after they'd given Yvonne Knight her promised photograph, Joycie had whisked them into her private parlor, turned on the television, and hovered over them while they surfed the various newscasts. The main story on all stations was Milton Ryce's suspicious death.

"It's you, Inspector!" exclaimed Joycie, as a shot of Carol appeared on the screen. "And there's my hotel! And the Town Hall! This is *excellent*." She bustled for the door, saying over her shoulder, "Forgive me for leaving you, but it's imperative I contact the Hash's Creek tourism bureau and make sure they're gearing up to take advantage of this publicity bonanza."

The network station owning the DVD images of Ryce's "death plunge," as they called it, predictably ran the footage several times with a voice-over making entirely superfluous comments in a suitably shocked tone. The first frame showed Milton Ryce as a speck in the sky, then, with shocking suddenness, the speck became a recognizable human being, hurtling toward the ground.

Other stations, denied this sensational material, had concentrated on interviewing Sergeant Huffner—who swelled with self-importance at every question—and tracking down family members, business acquaintances and the very few victims of Ryce's practical jokes who were willing to appear on camera.

There were long shots of Ted Ryce in front of Ryce Hall, obviously taken with a telephoto lens from outside the property; society footage of the wife of the deceased, Deanna, at a charity event; followed by a view of the facade of the Ryce mansion in Sydney where the widow was "in grieving seclusion."

"Where is Rae Ryce?" portentously inquired one smooth young man behind a news desk. A still photograph appeared on the screen, showing Rae squinting malevolently into the camera. "Rae is the only daughter of Milton Ryce, whose death on Saturday in what seemed a terrible skydiving accident, is now being investigated as something more sinister . . ."

The screen returned to the young man, who intoned meaningfully, "Rae Ryce's present whereabouts are unknown. When the brokenhearted daughter is located, we'll be first to bring you the interview."

Bourke had cynically remarked, "It is, after all, the main role of television interviewers to ferret out grief-stricken relatives to inquire: 'How do you feel?'"

"We don't know Rae Ryce *is* grief-stricken."

"Money soothes heartache, you mean?" Bourke asked mockingly.

"Something like that," said Carol. "'Follow the money' is not a bad idea in cases like this."

"Ryce was pretty well universally loathed, so gaining dollars from his death may not be the prime motive. Anyone who worked with him, or for him, people he humiliated with his elaborate jokes . . . the list of suspects is getting longer by the minute."

"Even so," said Carol, "you know as well as I do it's usually the nearest and dearest who carry out the deed."

"Larry Frobisher could fill that bill. He seems to have stuck to Ryce like a leech."

Carol had laughed at Bourke's acid tone. "You really don't like him, do you?"

"*Obnoxious* is the first word that comes to mind," Bourke had said, adding with a grin, "Not that I won't be totally fair and impartial when investigating the little creep."

THE CLEMENT ESTATE, announced the polished brass plate affixed to a fluted column holding one of the two rampant stone lions guarding the entrance. A heavy steel gate barred the way. A media van was already parked by the side of the road, and a small cluster of people were arguing with a stolid ox of a man in a gray uniform.

He broke away from them to approach Carol and Bourke's car. "Inspector Ashton? You're expected. I'll let you through."

The media group convulsed. A cameraman swung his camera

up to his shoulder. The reporter, obvious from his suit among the others in jeans, set off toward them clutching a microphone, sound technician in tow.

The guard activated the gate. At Carol's instruction, before driving through, Bourke leaned out of his window. "Mate, just a question."

"Anything to help the police," said the guard, tongue in cheek.

"Rae Ryce? I presume you know her?"

"Sure. She often visits."

"She stayed here last night?"

The man nodded warily. "Yeah, she did, but she's not there now."

"What time did Ms. Ryce arrive yesterday?"

He shrugged. "Dunno for sure. Late afternoon, around six, six-thirty."

"And when did she leave this morning?" Bourke asked.

The guard made a face. "Too bloody early. Got me out of bed to open the gate. Around five-thirty, I reckon."

The reporter reached them. "Inspector Ashton! Just a few words."

"Shove off," said the guard. "This is private property."

Bourke accelerated smoothly through the gate, leaving the gesticulating reporter behind. "They'll still be here when we leave," he said. "Beats me how those media types do their jobs. I'd go mad, just waiting around for hours hoping something newsworthy will happen or someone will arrive. You have to be a pushy, patient type to do it."

"This is mild stuff, nothing like it'll be back in Sydney." Carol had been in the spotlight many times with high-profile cases, but she still marveled at the resolve and persistence of members of the media who rarely took no for an answer, pursuing stories with bulldog tenacity.

The curving drive brought them to a startling sight. The edifice was an extraordinarily large, blindingly white Italian villa. The balustrades of its three floors held rows of white urns, each overflowing with bright blossoms. On either side of the building arbors groaned with the burden of ornamental grapevines.

One half of the double front door opened and Basil Clement strolled out to meet them. He was wearing a crisp white shirt, tailored slacks and undoubtedly expensive slip-on leather shoes. The glare of publicity in which he continually basked had made his tanned, handsome face very familiar to Carol, but in the unforgiving light he looked much older than she'd expected. Lines fanned from the corners of his eyes and his mouth was deeply bracketed. As a champion golfer, he'd always been trim and athletic, but the sweet life he'd enjoyed since he'd left the sport had thickened his waistline and coarsened his features. When he came closer, she could see the broken capillaries in his nose that often indicated a heavy drinker.

"Inspector Ashton," he said, smiling broadly as he offered his hand. "Welcome to my villa."

Carol introduced Bourke, and Clement shook hands with him, too. Then, with a sweep of his arm, he indicated the building. "What do you think of it?"

Bourke remained diplomatically silent. Carol said, "Impressive."

Clement gave a satisfied grunt. "It is, isn't it? Entirely my design, inside and out. And the grounds, too, of course. An architect did the plans to my specifications. What you see before you is all my work. I often think it's a pity I didn't choose a career as an architect. I believe I would have had a lot to offer."

Carol nodded politely. This was encouragement enough for Basil Clement to continue. "I'm building a splendid house in Sydney overlooking Palm Beach. I've designed every little detail of the structure, directing the architect to specify only the best of everything, no matter what it costs. Huge windows, magnificent views of the ocean and Barrenjoey Lighthouse. You know the area? It's magnificent, isn't it?"

Squinting in the reflected light from the white walls of the villa before them, Bourke asked, "Is the house in this style?"

"No, not at all. One villa's enough. I hope I don't sound too arrogant when I say I'm inventing my *own* style, rather like Frank Lloyd Wright did. My building will be something individually, unmistakably Basil Clement."

"We do have some questions, Mr. Clement," Carol said in a firm, let's-get-down-to-business tone.

"Of course, of course. Come in. And do call me Basil. I've never stood on formality, as you probably know."

A blast of frigid air-conditioned air hit them as they entered. Compared to the warm morning outside, it was almost too cold, and Carol regretted wearing the light short-sleeved suit she'd chosen from her meager traveling wardrobe.

"Morris is somewhere around. He'll want to meet you, I'm sure," said Clement, ushering them into a huge room with an ornately vaulted ceiling. The area was obviously used for entertaining. A gigantic mirrored bar took up one side. The opposite wall was entirely glass, looking out into the green of a luxurious fern garden. Seating was provided by clusters of lounges grouped around low tables, many of which held miniature renditions of famous sculptures. A large, sunken fish pool in the middle of the room held a collection of bright orange koi fish, which gathered on one side of the pool, as if to greet them.

"My babies," said Clement, smiling. "Aren't they beautiful? They love me. People don't realize that fish can feel affection." He looked inquiringly at Carol. "Were you aware of this, Inspector?"

"I must admit I've not heard that before."

"Nevertheless, it's true. See how they come to me?"

Bourke, unimpressed, said, "Might it have something to do with the fish expecting food?"

Clement didn't deign to reply to this. Pointedly addressing Carol, he said, "Perhaps you would care for some refreshments?"

"That's kind of you, Mr. Clement, but that's not necessary."

Indicating a lounge near the fish, he said, "Then let's sit here."

Once seated, Bourke took out his notebook. Basil Clement, with a wry smile, took a slim recorder from his pocket. "I hope you don't mind, Inspector, but I record all interviews. I've found, over the years, it's the only way to protect myself. I have all such conversations transcribed and filed."

"Perhaps you would provide me with a copy of this interview?" Carol said.

Clement seemed surprised, and then amused. "Of course."

"Yesterday, when I spoke to you, Mr. Clement," said Carol, "I asked you about Rae Ryce's whereabouts. You claimed you didn't know where she was. However, it has come to our attention that Ms. Ryce was, in fact, here. She spent the night, and left early this morning. I'm wondering why you found it necessary to lie to me."

"A lie, Inspector? That's a bit harsh." He tried a charming smile. "I was being a little over-protective, perhaps."

Carol's expression remained grave. "It's a serious matter to lie to the police."

He spread his hands. "Believe me, Inspector Ashton, I would normally answer every question with absolute truthfulness, but Rae's a bit of a damaged soul, you know. If I'd told you she was here, she'd have found it hard to forgive me."

His tone indulgent, he went on, "We do provide a bit of a bolt-hole for Rae at times. She's an impetuous kid, tending to sound off without thinking first. She's often been in conflict with her father, or, frankly, with any authority figure. However, Rae knows she's always welcome at the villa."

"Do you know where she's gone?" Carol asked.

"Back to her place in Sydney. She has a little cottage in Glebe, near Sydney University. It was a present from Milton for Rae's twenty-first birthday a few years back. I'll give you the address, if you don't have it."

"What about her brother, Ted?" Bourke asked. "Do you have much to do with him?"

Basil Clement came close to sneering. "As little as possible. Nasty piece of work. I'm assuming it was his handiwork on the news this morning. Huffner had told me Ted had filmed his father's death."

"You know Sergeant Huffner?" said Bourke.

"Of course. This is a country town. You get to know everyone the way you never could in the city. Part of the charm of Hash's Creek."

"And do you know Larry Frobisher?" Bourke asked.

This elicited a wide grin from Basil. "I should say so! I've kept the little guy supplied with gossip items for years."

"Mr. Frobisher paid you for them?"

His grin disappeared. "Of course not," he said coldly. "They're items about *me*." He cheered up to add, "If I say so myself, the public always seems interested in my comings and goings. The Lawrence Frobisher Report contains up-to-date news on celebrities, so it's natural Basil Clement would be included."

Cynically amused by the man's effortless self-absorption, exemplified by his reference to himself in the third person, Carol said, "Surely you don't approve of everything about you that appears on Frobisher's Web site."

"Everything? I should say not. But you know the old expression, 'No news is bad news.'"

"I rather thought the saying was, 'No news is good news,'" Carol said, raising an eyebrow.

Basil flapped his hand. "Whatever."

"A few months ago the Frobisher Report ran an item about an altercation you had with Dr. Gilbert Edmundson," said Carol.

Basil flapped his hand again. "It was a non-event. I have to confess I'd been drinking, and Edmundson said something I took exception to—a remark about washed-up sports heroes. I took a swing at him. There was nothing more to it than that."

"Mr. Frobisher claims to have been involved in the planning and execution of a practical joke for Milton Ryce," said Bourke. "Do you know anything about it?"

"There's not much gets past me," declared Basil Clement with pride. "I believe the hoax Larry worked on was the bunyip myth. You know, the monster in the night scaring people camping in the wilderness. An American network even sent out a team to film a special called *Australia's Big Foot*. Milton had them totally fooled when his so-called world-renowned experts identified the footprints and droppings as belonging to a great ape, thought to be extinct for millions of years."

"Mr. Ryce appeared to have enjoyed embarrassing the media," Carol observed.

"He enjoyed embarrassing *everybody*."

"Were you ever a target for a practical joke?" Bourke asked.

Basil seemed astonished by the question. "Me fall for a practical joke? No way. I'm too sharp. Milton knew that. He'd never try anything on me."

"You were expecting Mr. Ryce and Ms. Watson for lunch on Saturday," Carol said.

Basil nodded agreement. "Morris and I were so looking forward to seeing them both. Milton was always entertaining, and Kym . . ." His smile almost a leer, he added, "A very attractive young woman, I'm sure you'll agree."

"We've interviewed Ms. Watson," said Bourke.

"Then you see what I mean."

"Have you known Kymberly Watson long?" Carol asked.

"Only a few months. She was Milton's latest . . . interest. I believe they met while at some skydiving convention."

Bourke glanced up from his notebook. "Are you into skydiving yourself?"

Clement shuddered. "Christ, no! I can't stand heights at the best of times. The thought of jumping out of a plane makes me literally sick to the stomach. Milton persuaded my brother to try it once, but there's no way he could ever persuade me."

"On Saturday, were there other guests?" Carol asked.

"No, just the four of us. When Milton and Kym were late arriving, I knew something serious had happened. Milton was always punctual."

As he was speaking, Carol became aware that someone was standing just inside the door, unobtrusively listening. Basil Clement followed the direction of her gaze. "Morris, what are you lurking over there for? Come and meet Inspector Ashton and . . ."

"Sergeant Bourke," Carol supplied.

Morris Clement walked slowly over to them, as though he was treading on a treacherous surface. Although in looks very like his brother, he had none of Basil's joviality. Morris moved with shoulders slightly hunched, and his pale, set face was a contrast to Basil Clement's weather-beaten, mobile features. Nor was Morris as well-dressed. He wore a faded, red-striped shirt, baggy blue tracksuit pants and grubby running shoes.

He nodded to Carol and Bourke, obviously not intending to do anything as formal as shaking hands, then, with every sign of reluctance, obeyed his brother's impatient gesture and sat down where Basil indicated.

"Morris and I were shattered when we heard Milton had died." Basil looked over at his brother for confirmation, but Morris remained impassive. Basil frowned, then continued, "Initially, I couldn't believe it was true. I kept expecting Milton to walk through the door, laughing because everyone had fallen for yet another one of his outrageous hoaxes."

"I believe the early media reports suggested it might be a ruse," said Carol.

Basil shook his head ruefully. "The funny thing is, Milton would have been quite capable of setting such a thing up, had he thought of it. He enjoyed a good practical joke more than anyone."

Morris Clement spoke for the first time. "It seems this time the joke's on Milton, wouldn't you say?"

Chapter Eight

"What did you think of the Clement brothers?" Carol asked, as Bourke waited for the villa's entrance gate to open.

"They're polar opposites. Basil is an extroverted attention-seeker. Morris seems the glum sort. Except for that acid remark about the joke being on Ryce, he hardly said two words." He added, sarcastically, "Of course, Basil took up the slack. As self-centered as they come. That guy's someone I'd get tired of fast."

As soon as they were through the gate, the waiting television crew, who'd been lounging in the shade of an overhanging tree, sprang into action. Carol kept her face blank as Bourke drove past, knowing she was on camera. It was likely the footage would never be used, unless later the Clement brothers became suspects. If that happened, Carol and Bourke's departure from the Clement estate would become newsworthy.

"Do we add Basil and Morris to the suspect list, Mark?"

"There's no obvious motive. And would either of them know enough about skydiving equipment to disable a parachute?"

"Basil Clement said his brother was persuaded by Ryce to make a parachute jump. You might check that with Bendix." Her phone trilled.

She spoke for a few moments, then disconnected. "It's confirmed—the Air Force agrees with the APF. Deliberate sabotage of both Ryce's main and reserve chutes, and the same for Verity Stuart's main parachute. One interesting thing, though. In the case of Ryce, the lines to the canopies were cut, so when he pulled the ripcord, each was released but was then useless. The Stuart parachute was more sophisticated. The ripcord itself was disabled, so the canopy wouldn't deploy at all."

"That makes sense," said Bourke. "Milton Ryce was a very experienced skydiver, so he'd know just what to do without the trouble of unpacking the parachute to cut the lines."

"This is going to limit the list of suspects," said Carol. "First, someone has to have access to Ryce's gear, and second, the person has to know how to repack the chutes once the damage has been done."

Bourke grinned at her. "But Carol, what if the murderer prepares the sabotaged gear at leisure, and switches packs at the last minute? What if he or she gets a copy of *Skydiving for Dummies*, and simply follows the easy, step-by-step directions?"

"I find it hard to believe there *is* such a book as *Skydiving for Dummies*," said Carol, laughing. "And if such a book exists, I very much doubt its contents include instructions on how to tamper with a parachute."

Bourke dropped Carol at the airport and left to return to Hash's Creek to pick up the search warrant for Ryce Hall, and then to meet with the technician from the company that had supplied Ryce's safe.

Before Carol's plane left for Sydney, she called Anne Newsome to ask her to locate Ian McNamara and Verity Stuart, and to verify Kymberly Watson's assertion that Deanna Ryce had been responsible for someone's death. Ryce's mistress had been irritatingly vague about the details of this purported killing, airily saying that it was just a rumor she'd heard somewhere, sometime.

And finally, if possible, Anne was to set up a meeting with Milton Ryce's widow.

Anne met Carol at Sydney Airport with the news that Deanna Ryce was only available for an hour that afternoon, so they would have to go directly to the Ryce house in Turramurra.

"As for the dark secret in Deanna Ryce's past," said Anne, "I can't find any record of her being involved in any fatality, deliberate or accidental, at least not in Australia. She was born in South Africa, and I've got a request in to search records there, but nothing's come back yet."

Anne went on to report that she'd checked on the flight plans submitted for trips from Sydney to Ryce's private airfield at Hash's Creek, and there were relatively few, and most had been filed by Bendix, Ryce's pilot.

As Anne drove, Carol checked herself out in the visor mirror. She looked and felt tired. She'd been hoping to have time to freshen up and change clothes before the interview.

Carol glanced over at her companion. Detective Constable Anne Newsome was as buoyantly vigorous as usual. Her skin glowed, her short curly hair shone, and, Carol thought with a touch of amused chagrin, her eyes positively sparkled. "Do you have to look so disgustingly healthy?" Carol inquired.

Anne grinned. "Sorry, boss. It's the genes, you know. Nothing to do with me. I lead a very unhealthy life."

"And that unhealthy life includes skydiving?"

"Mark told you, did he? I'm a rank beginner. Haven't had a solo drop yet."

Anne went on to describe how a friend—Carol surmised this was the new boyfriend Bourke had mentioned—had persuaded her to join a skydiving club. "The weekend before last we did a tandem free-fall. It was great! Someone else is there to make sure everything goes okay, and you can just enjoy the experience."

"No way would I be stepping out of a plane into thin air," said Carol. "How high up were you when you did this?"

"Four thousand feet—it sounds more impressive than thirteen hundred meters. Lance and I had about a forty-second free-fall, then the parachutes opened for a five-minute ride to the ground. It was fantastic."

"How heavy is the equipment?"

"When you're all suited up, it's reasonably heavy. About twelve kilograms. But once you're falling, you don't notice any weight at all, until you feel the jerk of the canopy opening."

"*If* it opens."

Anne laughed. "It's pretty safe. They tell me only one in eighty-two thousand skydives is fatal. Now, take BASE jumping. That's a whole different story. One in a thousand die indulging in that sport."

Much earlier in Carol's career, she'd arrested a man who'd parachuted off the arch of the Sydney Harbour Bridge, so she knew what the acronym BASE referred to: Buildings, Antennas, Spans (bridges), and Earth (cliffs). Wearing specially designed parachutes, BASE jumpers hurled themselves off such heights for the psychological and physical rush that extreme risk-taking gave them.

"Anne, promise me you won't entertain even the idea of BASE jumping."

"I wouldn't dream of it. Ordinary skydiving is hairy enough for me."

Anne, who had only glanced at a street directory before they set off, had enviable navigation skills. Without hesitation, she turned off the main road into a maze of streets. "We're almost there. It's somewhere near the crest of this hill," she said, negotiating a sharp bend.

She finally drew up outside a large but not conspicuously luxurious house. As at Ryce Hall, there were no obvious security measures. Manicured grass ran down to the road, there was no front fence or gate, and they were free to enter the circular driveway.

All in black, as befitted a new widow, Deanna Ryce, nee Lustgarten, opened the door to them. She exuded graceful style from her neat cap of black hair to her elegant high heels. Her makeup was flawless, her expression pensive. Her jewelry consisted of plain pearl earrings, a diamond watch and a wide gold wedding ring.

"Inspector Ashton. Please come in." She led the way to a comfortable sitting room, plainly furnished. The most notable point in the room was a huge alabaster vase full of deep red roses.

Carol introduced Anne Newsome, then began with her standard commiserations for Deanna Ryce's loss.

After listening with polite attention, she said, "I'm not going to pretend inconsolable grief, Inspector Ashton. I imagine you already know Milton and I were discussing divorce." She had a slight, clipped accent Carol wouldn't have recognized as South African, had she not known Deanna had been born there.

"Only discussing?" Carol said. "You hadn't initiated proceedings?"

"We'd talked to our respective lawyers." A faint, frosty amusement touched her face. "Both are very expensive gentlemen who smacked their lips at the prospect of a battle royal over every possible item. Milton could afford to make concessions, but he hated to lose. It was going to be a long, protracted battle."

"I must tell you," said Carol, "we're now investigating your husband's death as a homicide." Anne looked up from her notebook, obviously interested to see what reaction this news would bring.

"You really believe Milton was murdered?" Deanna Ryce's face was expressionless, but there was the slightest tremor in her voice. Carol wondered what thoughts and feelings were boiling beneath her cool exterior.

"The Air Force experts confirm the Australian Parachute Federation findings. Both parachutes had lines deliberately cut."

She grimaced. "How dreadful."

"Unless Mr. Ryce cut them himself, we—"

"Not suicide," Deanna said emphatically. "Milton would never kill himself."

Carol nodded. "That seems to be the general opinion, so we're interested in anyone who could conceivably have a reason to murder your husband. Does any particular person come to mind?"

"Milton thrived on conflict." She rose gracefully. "Would you come with me?"

They followed her out into the hallway. Pausing beside a paneled door, she said, "Perhaps you'd like to view what Milton called his Sucker Gallery."

She ushered them into a long, rectangular room bare of any furniture, save for four heavily padded benches situated so one could view each wall from a comfortable seat.

Photographs, pages from newspapers and other materials were exhibited as if they were valuable artworks. Flat-screen monitors were part of most displays. Some presentations merited a major position on a wall. Others were grouped with lesser specimens in a collage.

Deanna indicated the nearest display. "Milton's most recent triumph." Her tone was caustic.

"The flying saucer hoax," said Anne, examining the presentation closely.

"Poor Richie Keele," Deanna said with feeling, "I imagine it will take a long time for him to live it down."

The tennis player's humiliation had been very public. In the world of professional tennis, Richie Keele was rated in the top ten. The skills that made him a superior athlete had been of no assistance when Milton Ryce decided Keele would be the victim of one of his infamous hoaxes.

Punching a button to activate the display's monitor, Deanna said, "As I'm sure you're aware, Milton always made sure he had a comprehensive visual record of each person's mortification. He enjoyed reliving his achievements."

On the screen Richie Keele's familiar face appeared. He was saying, with barely-repressed excitement, "I've called this media conference today because I have the most incredible news. With my own eyes, I've seen a UFO, up close and personal! And I have photographic proof and material taken from the space ship. I'm not talking about a simple light-in-the-sky sighting. I've been privileged to experience a real encounter with something extraterrestrial, something from beyond our solar system!"

It had long been common knowledge that Keele was a supporter of SETI, the Search for Extraterrestrial Intelligence. He'd not only given financial support to the organization, he'd also been active in publicizing SETI's drive to link private desktop computers in a gigantic web of computing power to analyze the spectrum of electronic signals raining down on Earth from space. Keele was on record as saying he believed many UFO sightings were credible and that government cover-ups were common.

Given Keele's active interest in such things, he was frequently approached by people who claimed to have seen flying saucers or been abducted by aliens. When a trim, middle-aged man with a military bearing turned up with official-looking documents he claimed to have smuggled out from a covert government department devoted to investigating UFO sightings, Richie Keele was already predisposed to believe the story.

Introducing himself as Charles Moore, a former member of the secret department, he told Keele how he'd become deeply disgusted at the concealment of such vital facts from the public. The man—actually an actor paid by Ryce—had explained it was only through trusted celebrities like Richie Keele that the truth could be revealed.

Totally convinced that Charles Moore was genuine, Keele avidly read the documents. They seemed authentic, describing an incredible, but plausible scenario. UFOs not only existed, but over the years several had crashed on Australian territory and had been recovered, although all alien crew members had been killed. The government had categorized all information about extraterrestrial contacts as top secret. Moore explained how on those occasions when ordinary people witnessed anything to do with genuine

UFOs, an undercover bureau, specifically set up to discredit such witnesses, immediately went into action.

Moore told Richie Keele that the federal government had a scheme to use a captured UFO to lure other extraterrestrials into a rescue mission by activating the spaceship's emergency beacon. It just so happened, Moore said, that he knew the exact location of the crashed spaceship in virgin bushland, as well as the night the distress signal would be turned on. If Keele would come with him and be a witness to the skullduggery, together they could then go to the media and reveal the government's duplicity.

Richie Keele fell for it. He had bought camouflage clothing and hiking boots to trek through the bush to where the spaceship had gone down, and equipped himself with night vision binoculars, a camera suitable for poor light and a state-of-the-art camcorder.

Milton Ryce appeared on the screen to explain the finer points of his hoax. The creation of the illusion had taken detailed planning and the application of considerable money and personnel. On the appointed night, in undeveloped bushland, the deception began with weird lights in the sky, leading Moore and Keele to a site deep in the bush, mocked-up by a film crew to resemble a crashed UFO.

An astounding scene greeted Richie Keele. Supposed extraterrestrials—actually dwarfs disguised as aliens—carried dim, diffuse lights to illuminate their progress as they made their way toward the crashed ship. Keele had the presence of mind to activate the camcorder he was carrying, not knowing that he, himself, was being professionally filmed. Then, pandemonium broke as actors dressed in military uniforms attacked the aliens and carried them away into the night.

Moore had allowed Richie Keele to retrieve a piece of strangely marked metal from the crashed UFO, then they had, at Moore's urging, left the area, purportedly to avoid arrest by returning military forces.

Overjoyed to have the "proof" of the existence of UFOs and the cover-up carried on by the government, Keele broadcast the news through every medium available. He was very convincing, because he totally believed what he was saying.

Every step of this elaborate practical joke had been recorded, including Richie Keele's final, red-faced public mortification when the deception was revealed.

A beaming Milton Ryce appeared at the end of the presentation to say, "I'm sure you'll agree, this has been one of my most successful hoaxes."

Expressionless, Deanna snapped off the screen. "As you can see, Inspector, my husband made an art form out of alienating people and turning them into bitter enemies." She glanced around the room. "I imagine more than one person featured here hated Milton enough to kill him."

"Did anyone openly threaten him?"

"Many people did, some in disturbingly violent detail. Milton never paid any attention."

"Is it possible to get a list of hoax victims?" Anne asked.

"That's easily done." Deanna added sardonically, "My husband kept excellent records. I can't fault him there."

Carol said, "It's been mentioned to us that in the past you were involved in someone's death."

Deanna Ryce's blank face was suddenly suffused with anger. "No doubt Kymberly Watson is your source for this information," she snapped.

"You know Ms. Watson?"

Carol's question elicited a grim smile. "Perhaps you thought, Inspector, I wouldn't be on speaking terms with my husband's lover."

"We'd been led to understand that was the case," Carol said.

Her manner more animated, Deanna said, "Kym Watson approached me. I certainly would never have got in touch with her. Had the bare-faced effrontery to come here, while Milton was overseas on business, to try a little gentle blackmail."

"Ms. Watson threatened you openly?"

Deanna gave a contemptuous laugh. "Too clever for that. She

was careful how she phrased it, but it was perfectly clear the woman expected a substantial monetary reward for keeping quiet about what she called, tactfully, 'an unfortunate incident.' She was less than pleased when I said I wouldn't pay a cent for her silence. I told her that, as far as I was concerned, she could tell Milton whatever she liked."

"*Did* Ms. Watson tell your husband?"

"I've no idea, Inspector. I doubt Milton would have cared, anyway." Her mouth tightened. "I imagine she couldn't wait to spill the beans to you. I'm sure Kym Watson's been looking to make trouble for me ever since I refused to play along with her blackmail attempt."

"I'm afraid we need details of the incident that led her to believe you could be blackmailed."

Deanna gusted a sigh. "All right, Inspector, I'll tell you. I was born and grew up in South Africa. It happened when I was young, hadn't had my license for long. I don't drink alcohol—don't like the taste—so I was often the driver designated to get people home after parties. This one night we'd all been to a particularly raucous birthday celebration. It was dark, and perhaps I was distracted by the merriment in the car. Whatever the reason, I didn't see the man until his body was thrown up by the force of the impact to break the windscreen in front of me."

"How seriously injured was he?"

She dropped her head. "He died instantly. I should have been charged with manslaughter, careless driving—something. A man had been killed. However, my father was very influential. He pulled just the right strings and the whole incident was hushed up. The man who died was an habitual drunk, but that didn't excuse it. Nevertheless, I went along with the cover-up. My father arranged for a substantial sum to be paid to the family. Then my parents told me to go on like it never happened. To forget it."

She looked directly at Carol, as though seeking absolution. "You deal with death so often, Inspector. Perhaps you understand how I would have liked more than anything to put it behind me, to wipe out the heavy, meaty thud as his body hit the windscreen. Blood, and shattered glass and someone screaming—me, I think. After all these years, at times I still dream about it . . ."

"Apart from your parents, who knew about this?"

She shook her head. "A few officials, probably long gone now. And my friends who were passengers in the car, but I've lost contact with them over the years. No one else. That's why it's such a puzzle how Kymberly found out. I asked her, of course, but she just shrugged and said something about how the dead never stay buried."

"When you give Constable Newsome the list of your husband's hoax victims, would you also provide all the necessary information about the time and place of the accident, plus any names you remember."

"Of course."

Noticing Deanna had become very white, Carol said, "Are you okay?"

"I don't like this room, Inspector. It shows the mean, vindictive side of Milton." With a faint smile, she added, "And yes, though seldom seen, at times there was a much nicer side to my husband. Actually, I first met him in the hospice ward of a children's hospital, where I was visiting my niece. Milton always kept it secret, but he gave not only money but a great deal of his time to children suffering with life-threatening diseases."

Carol saw Anne's eyebrows rise. The young constable was no doubt finding this facet of Ryce's life as unlikely as Carol did.

Deanna had moved to the door. "Do you mind if we go back to the sitting room? Unless the interview is over . . . ?"

"Just a few more questions," said Carol smoothly.

Once seated in the sitting room, Carol asked, "Have you tried skydiving yourself?"

"Milton persuaded me to jump a couple of times, in tandem—I never graduated to solo. I didn't particularly enjoy the experience, and Milton eventually accepted that I wasn't going to share his hobby."

"Your husband packed his own parachutes before a jump?"

90

"Invariably. He wouldn't trust anyone else to do it."

"Did he usually pack them here, or at Ryce Hall?"

She indicated the door. "He'd either spread everything along the carpet outside in the hallway, and pack the chutes here in Sydney, or do it up at the Hall's airfield, where there's a room set up with long tables for just that purpose."

"Last weekend, where did he pack his equipment?"

Deanna raised her shoulders in an elegant shrug. "Frankly, I've no idea. I lost all interest in Milton's affairs long ago." A cold smile appeared as she said, "Even the one he was carrying on with Kym Watson was of no concern to me."

Carol leaned forward confidingly. "You can see why this is a key question," she said. "Someone had to have access to the equipment in order to sabotage it."

Deanna spread her hands. "I wouldn't have the faintest idea what to do, and even if I had, I can't imagine what it would take to knowingly send someone to such a horrible death."

"I believe your husband drove to Hash's Creek last weekend, instead of flying. Do you know if he had a passenger?"

"Inspector, how can I make myself plain? We lived separate lives. I don't know and I don't care."

Carol said, "You know Ian McNamara well?"

She stiffened. "Ian? He's one of Milton's business associates."

"Is he a friend of yours?"

Deanna put her chin up. "Are you implying anything, Inspector?"

"We're interested in everyone who saw your husband last weekend. Mr. McNamara was on the plane. He jumped first, landed safely, and then witnessed your husband's fall."

"You can't think Ian would do something like that." Her pale face flushed. Her voice rising, she said, "It's an outrageous suggestion!"

"We have to ask these questions, Ms. Ryce."

"I understand." Her hands fluttered. "It's just a shock to think someone I know might have done this to Milton."

Carol noticed how interested Anne was in Deanna Ryce's loss

of composure. It intrigued Carol, too. To increase the pressure, Carol said, "We've been advised that prior to your marriage you signed a prenuptial agreement."

Deanna tugged at one discreet pearl earring. "So? That's standard with wealthy men these days."

"The agreement is null and void now your husband is dead?"

Taking a furious breath, Deanna fixed Carol with a piercing glare. "That's right, Inspector Ashton. And I inherit approximately half the estate. Are you aware that Ted and Rae get a quarter each? It's a lot of money—millions. So why aren't you questioning *them*?"

"We've spoken to your stepson. We can't find Rae Ryce."

"Rae called me just before you arrived. She's at Gilbert Edmundson's clinic."

"That surprises me," said Carol. "From all accounts your stepdaughter was actively resisting treatment from Dr. Edmundson."

"Rae changes from minute to minute. One day she's declaring Gilbert is a charlatan, the next he's the most wonderful psychiatrist in the world." Deanne added dryly, "Apparently at the moment Gil is a candidate for sainthood. Tomorrow Rae may declare he's the devil."

"I notice you refer to him as Gil," Carol said.

"I count him as a friend," she said shortly. Rising, she checked her watch. "I'm sorry, Inspector, I have another appointment. Funeral arrangements. I'll give the information you requested to your constable, then I'm afraid I have to leave."

"One thing—I believe a Mr. Boyne was employed as your chauffeur."

"He's no longer in my employ."

"He left voluntarily?"

Deanna Ryce gave Carol a long look. "He was fired for dishonesty, Inspector. I don't wish to say anything more."

"Do you have an address?"

She made an impatient gesture. "I have no idea where he is. I must go."

Carol and Anne got to their feet. Carol said, "Thank you for your time, Ms. Ryce. I may have further questions . . ."

Deanna made a gesture akin to brushing away an annoying insect. "Naturally I'll cooperate." She paused. "Will you be present at Milton's funeral, Inspector? It's scheduled for Thursday afternoon."

"I intend to be there, unless you have some objection."

"So it's true? You actually believe murderers attend their victims' funerals? I thought it was just in mystery novels that happened."

"The majority of murders are committed by family or close friends," Carol said. "This makes it a distinct possibility the person responsible for your husband's death will be at the funeral, not necessarily to gloat, but because his or her absence would be notable."

"Kym Watson's absence from the funeral is something you might note," said Deanna, her tone acid. "I don't believe even she would have the audacity to attend." She added with a vicious smile, "Please tell me you have that little bitch at the very top of your list of suspects."

A few minutes later, climbing into the car, Carol said to Anne, "Mark predicted Deanna Ryce would try to make Kym Watson the prime suspect."

"*Is* Kym Watson near the top of your list?"

Carol laughed. "Anne," she said, "there's a multitude positively jostling to be first in line!"

Chapter Nine

As Anne drove with her customary smooth skill, Carol called a number Sergeant Huffner had provided and Anne had verified. "Ms. Stuart? This is Detective Inspector Carol Ashton . . . Yes, I understand how upset you must be . . . A dreadful experience . . . Just a brief meeting . . . Thank you, I have your address."

Verity Stuart lived in Woolloomooloo, historically a working-class inner city suburb servicing harborside docks. Now, slowly gentrifying, it sat uneasily between the grassy open expanses of the Domain and the condescending regard of fashionable Potts Point. Nearby, as if to add spice to the mix, was the racy Kings Cross district.

The address was in the middle of a row of narrow-fronted, rather dilapidated terrace houses, huddled together as if for support. With difficulty, Anne found a parking spot on an adjacent street, then she and Carol approached the peeling purple paint of Verity Stuart's front door.

Opening the door before they could use the tarnished brass knocker, a slightly-built woman with long black hair flowing loose on her shoulders said, in challenging tones, "Are you Inspector Ashton?"

Carol agreed she was, introduced Anne, and waited to be invited inside. For a moment it seemed Verity Stuart intended to answer questions while Carol and Anne stood in the tiny veranda area, separated from the street by a rusty cast iron fence, but at last she stood aside and gestured for them to enter.

"Go straight through. There's a courtyard at the back. We can have a private conversation there."

The narrow house had a wallpapered hallway running the length of the building, with a series of rooms opening off to the right. The inside of the house was in far better condition than the exterior, and the choice of furniture showed someone with a discerning eye for quality. The hall terminated at a small, modernized kitchen. An open door led out into the greenery of a tiny area, delineated on one side by the house and the other three sides by tall brick walls painted pale ocher. The rear wall of the courtyard had a door, hard to see because it was the same ocher color. It was securely padlocked.

Verity Stuart indicated bench seats at a painted table. "Hope you'll be comfortable enough out here."

As Carol and Anne seated themselves, she went back into the kitchen, shortly reappearing with a circular tray holding plastic glasses embellished with daisies and a matching pitcher. "Homemade ginger beer," she said. "If you don't like it, I can get you water. Can't offer coffee or tea. Never touch caffeine, so there's none in the house."

Anne declined a drink, but to be polite, Carol accepted a glass of ginger beer, sipped, and found it surprisingly good. "Lovely little courtyard," she said, glancing around. The floor was terracotta tiles and a little fountain had water playing over the shape of a naked cupid posed with bow and arrow at the ready.

Verity Stuart inclined her head in acknowledgment of the compliment. While she poured herself a glass of ginger beer, Carol assessed her.

She seemed in her mid-thirties. Her long, dark hair fell straight, framing her plain, serious face. Her eyes were deep, liquid brown, and she had a determined, thin-lipped mouth. She was wearing a scoop-necked floral top, faded blue jeans and high-heeled sandals.

"I've been listening to the news. It's on every station. He didn't die an accidental death, did he, Inspector?"

"It appears to be murder or suicide, Ms. Stuart."

She pursed her lips. "Milton was certainly capable of suicide."

Carol's eyebrows rose. "You're the first person to say so. The general consensus seems to be that Mr. Ryce would never kill himself."

"He was such a bastard, setting up all those cruel tricks to embarrass people. It's a wonder to me he could endure waking up every morning, knowing he had another day to live with himself."

Carol half-smiled. "A novel point of view, Ms. Stuart."

Verity Stuart's bleak expression didn't change. "I mean it," she said. "Milton was a noxious human being, full of self-hatred. I wouldn't put it past him to kill himself just to spite me."

She glanced at Anne, then down at Anne's notebook. "You're taking this down? Let me spell it out for you. On a personal level, I'm glad Milton Ryce is dead. On a professional level, I very much regret his passing."

"How is that?" Carol asked.

"I'm not telling you anything you won't find out soon enough, Inspector. Milton and I were partners on a project to develop these terraces. They're all rentals, and I have an option to buy the whole row from the owner. Milton and I planned a complete renovation—rewiring, new plumbing, refurbished kitchens and bathrooms—then we planned to sell each one individually. We would have made a considerable profit. I've done several makeovers with houses myself, doing them up and selling at a hefty return, but this was a much more ambitious scheme. I needed Milton to bankroll me."

"Did this scheme come up before or after you joined Leapers Anonymous?"

"After I'd joined. I won't lie to you, Inspector. I stayed in the club because Milton and I were business partners. I found him more and more repugnant as a person, but essential to me as far as this project was concerned."

"What's the situation now that Mr. Ryce is dead?"

Verity's mouth twisted. "The situation?" she said bitterly. "The whole thing will fall through."

"Surely there's alternative financing."

"It's not likely I can swing it on my own." Verity's fingers tapped a nervous tattoo on the table. "I'm not happy discussing this further. It's nobody's concern but mine. The only reason I mentioned the project in the first place is because I knew you'd be snooping around my affairs."

"Then let's switch subjects to skydiving last Saturday."

Verity shot Carol a furious glance. "Last Saturday I was set up! Milton let me jump from that plane knowing I had only one working parachute. If the reserve had failed, I'd have been killed. You've checked my gear, I'm sure, and have found someone got at it."

"That's correct," said Carol. "Who packed your parachute?"

"It must have been Milton."

"I gather most people in Leapers Anonymous pack their own," Carol remarked.

Verity shook her head. "Not me. It's not a skill I've ever acquired."

"When did you realize who was responsible for the tampering?"

"Ted was there at the drop zone with his bloody camcorder. Seeing his father die in front of his eyes had taken some of the steam out of him, but he still managed to make some crack about me panicking when my main chute didn't work. Afterwards, when

97

I talked to Ian on the drive back to Sydney, he said Ted had told him Milton had fixed my main chute so it wouldn't open."

Almost spluttering with indignation, she went on, "It was a practical joke, Ian said. Jesus! A *joke*!"

"Sergeant Huffner told us you were very upset."

"For a few moments I was convinced I was going to die! And then, when the reserve opened, and I got safely down, I saw what had happened to Milton. That could have been me! I'm not ashamed to say I threw up."

Carol asked her about Ryce's gear and if Verity knew where it had been packed.

"His stuff was already in the back of the Land Rover when we drove up from Sydney."

Hiding her surprise that Verity Stuart had been the passenger in Ryce's vehicle and not Kymberly Watson, Carol said, "The packs look very similar?"

"Milton's stuff is always top of the line, and cost him thousands. I settled for something less expensive, but yes, the chutes when packed look similar."

"Could someone have switched them, so Mr. Ryce got the faulty parachutes?"

Verity hooked strands of dark hair behind her ears. "I suppose," she said, "but isn't it *your* job, Inspector, to find out what happened?"

"You traveled to Hash's Creek by road with Milton Ryce last Friday. Were you the only passenger?"

"Yes."

"Wouldn't it have been easier to fly?"

"We had a lot to talk over. No one knew about our business partnership, and we liked it that way. There were problems: It looked like we were going to have a bit of trouble shifting some of the tenants here. Of course we were offering them substantial bonuses to vacate, but a few were being bloody-minded and holding out for more." She gave a sharp laugh. "Now they won't get anything. That'll wipe the smiles off their faces."

98

"Why would you keep your partnership secret, Ms. Stuart?"

Verity shrugged. "It was Milton's idea, not mine. He told me a divorce was on the cards. He was working hard to conceal as much of his wealth as possible. Our project was just one of his schemes."

"How well do you know his wife?"

"I wouldn't call us close friends."

"You dislike her?"

With narrowed eyes, Verity said, "Don't put words in my mouth. Deanna's a perfectly nice person, I'm sure, but we have nothing in common."

"Except Milton Ryce," Carol observed. "Did you know Deanna Ryce signed a prenuptial agreement?"

"I knew. Milton told me he'd had on good legal advice it could be broken. Said he wasn't going to sit by and let her lawyers milk him for millions."

She put up a hand. "Don't ask me who I think killed him, Inspector. I really don't know." She smiled grimly. "Though if you pushed me, I'd say Larry Frobisher. Milton had had it up to here with him, and was about to slap Frobisher with a defamation suit."

Back in the car, Carol punched in the number for the Inner Grace Clinic. She got to Gilbert Edmundson's personal assistant without difficulty, but then ran up against a wall of polite resistance.

"I'm very sorry, Inspector Ashton," the assistant said with professional regret, "but I can't see any space in Dr. Edmundson's schedule today, and tomorrow looks very tight, too. Perhaps Wednesday? I might be able to squeeze you in then."

"May I speak with Dr. Edmundson?"

"I'm sorry, Inspector, but he's asked for all his calls to be held. You might like to try tomorrow between twelve and one. He may be available then."

"What's your name, please?"

After a moment's pause, the woman said, "I'm Dr. Edmundson's personal assistant."

"I presume you have a name?" Carol's voice was dangerously cool. Out of the corner of her eye she saw Anne grin.

"Of course I do, Inspector. Helen Waite."

"Thank you, Ms. Waite. I'm investigating a suspicious death. Dr. Edmundson may be in possession of important information to do with the case. I don't imagine either Dr. Edmundson, or you, Ms. Waite, would relish being charged with obstructing a police investigation. I'll be at the clinic in twenty minutes."

"Please hold. I'll speak with Dr. Edmundson."

Anne, still grinning, said, "I'd say the good doctor will suddenly become available."

Her prediction was correct. Helen Waite came back on the line to say the doctor had been able to shuffle his appointments, and would be pleased to see Inspector Ashton at her convenience.

Although the clinic was close by, the early evening traffic was heavy, so it took all of the twenty minutes to get there. Carol took the opportunity to ring Sybil. Unless she'd gone for a swim—her house was situated near one of Sydney's stunning northern beaches—she should be there, probably looking out at her magnificent view and sipping a drink after a challenging day teaching English to migrant women.

As Carol listened to the phone ring she wondered why she was doing this. Surely it would be far more sensible to wait until this interview with Edmundson was over and she could go home to a hot shower and comfortable clothes. Carol was about to disconnect, when Sybil picked up the receiver.

"It's me," said Carol, suddenly conscious of the young constable sitting beside her.

"Carol?" Sybil sounded surprised. "Is everything okay?"

"Everything's fine." Now she had Sybil on the other end of the line, she wasn't quite sure what to say.

Sybil ended the pause that went on too long. "If you're calling about Aunt Sarah's party, she's already filled me in. I'm happy to pitch in and help, if you like."

"That would be great. Thank you."

Sybil chuckled, a warm sound that once had curled around Carol's heart. "Carol, I'll even volunteer to help her trim the list of guests to something manageable."

"Oh, please do," said Carol with deepest sincerity. "I'd be eternally grateful."

Another awkward pause. Carol broke it this time with, "There is one other thing. The portrait of Aunt Sarah. I know Yancey has it in an exhibition at the moment, but I'd love to borrow it as a centerpiece for the party."

Yancey Blake, Sybil's lover for the past year, was a renowned artist. She'd asked Carol's aunt to sit for her, and the result had been a luminous, extraordinary portrait. The Aunt Sarah who gazed from the frame was an essence of the real person, with all her irrepressible zest for life. Yancey had painted the background crowded with flora and fauna to honor Aunt Sarah's total commitment to saving the world's ecology.

"I thought you knew. Yancey and I have parted ways."

Carol had known, but she didn't feel inclined to tell Sybil that Yancey herself had asked to meet Carol in order to explain why the separation was occurring.

Feeling a little uncomfortable, Carol took the safest route, and responded with, "I'm sorry," and nothing more.

"I'll call Yancey and ask about the portrait."

Hearing the reluctance in Sybil's voice, Carol said quickly, "I hate to put you in an awkward position. Give me Yancey's number, and I'll contact her myself."

They had reached the street of the clinic's address. Carol said she had to go, apologized for interrupting Sybil's evening, and rang off.

Inner Grace Clinic was discreet. Perhaps that was the quality that had allowed Dr. Gilbert Edmundson to get around the inevitable objections from residents in this expensive Eastern Suburbs neighborhood, who could be expected to be unhappy at the prospect of having a center treating drug addicts, however rich or famous, in their exclusive area.

The clinic was concealed behind a high stone wall, and not even a glimpse could be gained from the road. There was an unobtrusive plate at the gate announcing INNER GRACE, with no mention of it being a medical facility. A tree-shrouded drive led to a well-proportioned two-story building notable for its blandness. The architect seemed to have been instructed to make sure that nothing of any character or interest should mar the simple facade of the plain brick structure. If the building had been a person, Carol thought, that person would be instantly forgettable.

Inside, however, the clinic resembled an elegant private hotel. The carpeting was thick, the furniture clearly expensive, the atmosphere one of hushed luxury. When Carol and Anne Newsome entered through the etched-glass doors, they were immediately greeted by a polished young woman with a careful smile who inquired in a low tone if she could help them in any way.

Informed that they had an appointment to meet with Dr. Edmundson, she made a quick call on to an extension, then flashed them a slightly wider smile to indicate they'd passed muster. "Helen will be with you in a moment."

Helen Waite appeared. She was as Carol had expected: a sleek young woman, impeccably groomed. Carol noticed with amusement that the personal assistant's welcoming smile was more a twitch of her lips, then her face became expressionless.

"Would you please follow me," she said. She took them to a small, beautifully appointed sitting room. "Dr. Edmundson will be with you directly."

"Doctors always like keep you waiting," said Anne, settling into an elegant chair with the air of one expecting to be there for some time. She'd just picked up a magazine, and said to Carol with astonishment that it was a current issue, when the doctor himself appeared to usher them into his office.

"So sorry you had difficulty getting to me, Inspector Ashton. At times one's staff can be a little too protective. I do hope you'll accept my apologies."

Carol had expected Gilbert Edmundson to be smoothly facile.

On television his resolute, hook-nosed face was frequently light-ened by a practiced flash of very white teeth. He was the perfect interviewee—always providing a crisp sound bite. Often to be found by the side of distressed celebrities as they tearfully announced substance abuse problems, Dr. Edmundson would end such appearances with an upbeat statement about his confidence there was no addiction that could not be overcome, once one put one's trust in the Inner Grace Clinic and its staff of caring, highly qualified medical professionals.

In person Carol found the man to be a lot less slick than she expected. His smile seemed more genuine and his statement that he'd help any way he could was delivered with apparent sincerity.

His office was austerely furnished in neutral shades. The only splash of color was in a still life on the wall behind the desk. It depicted a deep blue bowl overflowing with perfectly rendered peaches, so real that Carol could almost feel their furry skin and taste their delicious flesh.

He didn't retreat behind his desk, but seated Carol and Anne in comfortable lounge chairs and took the one opposite them him-self. "Helen said you'd mentioned a suspicious death. I presume you mean Milton's. As you must know, I arrived at the site just a few minutes after it happened. At the time I took it to be a dread-ful accident. Nothing more sinister."

"Further information has been provided that makes accidental death unlikely."

"You've ruled out suicide?"

"It seems unlikely," said Carol, "as we've been assured by sev-eral people who knew Mr. Ryce well that he would never take his own life. Do you agree with that view?"

"Milton and I have not been in a doctor-patient relationship, but yes, from my observations, I very much doubt suicide is an option." He rested his chin on his tented fingers. "Unless his sky-diving equipment was faulty, that leaves the unpalatable thought that someone deliberately killed him."

"I believe Ian McNamara called you to the scene."

Edmundson put down his hands and shook his head. "Poor Kym," he said. "She was literally distraught. Not surprising, after she'd witnessed such a tragedy."

"Is Ms. Watson a patient of yours?"

Edmundson gave Carol an understanding smile. "Inspector Ashton, I know you must ask these questions, but I must remind you of patient-doctor privilege."

"Is Ms. Watson your patient?"

"We're friends—acquaintances, really."

"So patient-doctor privilege doesn't apply."

Edmundson frowned. "I did supply medication to calm her down, so yes, I believe I could say Kym is my patient."

"You were aware she was Milton Ryce's mistress?"

"Mistress? What an old-fashioned word. At an educated guess, I'd say Frobisher told you that. He's the sort to use such a term. He fancies himself the sophisticate, you know, when he's really rather geeky, wouldn't you agree?"

Anne was busily taking notes, and Carol looked over to her. "That's Lawrence Frobisher, Anne."

"I'm sure you've heard of the little muckraker," Edmundson said to Anne.

Anne nodded. "The Lawrence Frobisher Report. I've seen it on the Web."

Edmundson seemed about to add something further on the subject, but before he could speak, Carol said, "Was it common knowledge that Kym Watson and Ryce were lovers?"

"Anyone who needed to know, knew."

"Does that include Ryce's wife?"

He shifted in his seat. "Naturally Deanna knew. Milton was one of those men who always had something going on the side. Deanna kept an eye on her rivals, just to make sure none of the affairs got too serious."

"Do you enjoy practical jokes, Dr. Edmundson?" Carol asked.

He pursed his lips, apparently deciding how to respond. "I abhor them, actually."

"But Milton Ryce loved them, didn't he?"

He made a face. "Milton had a vicious streak and the money to indulge it."

"Yet you were friends?"

"Our link was . . . professional."

"You were treating him?"

Edmundson sighed. "I suppose you'll dig until you find out. Milton's daughter, Rae, has had a substance abuse problem for some time. By sheer good fortune, she's never been arrested, so she has no police record. That's all I can say. I can't reveal any explicit details."

"What substances are you referring to, Dr. Edmundson?" Carol asked, impatient at his prevarication. "Alcohol? Prescription drugs? Illicit drugs? A combination of all the above?"

Edmundson's mouth tightened. "I believe it's not in Rae's best interests to discuss specifics, Inspector Ashton."

"We're not with the drug squad, doctor. We're investigating a possible murder. Specific details about Ms. Ryce's drug problems may well be pertinent to our inquiries." Carol softened her voice to add, "I'm not here to make trouble for her. If you can give me some guidance, off the record, I'd appreciate it."

After a pause for consideration, Edmundson said, "Off the record, mainly cocaine. Snorted, not injected. She has dabbled in a few designer drugs, ecstasy, for example."

"Meth? Heroin?"

He shook his head. "No, I don't believe so."

"Was it something to do with Rae that took you to Ryce Hall last weekend?"

Edmundson leaned back, apparently considering how to answer. At last he said, "Milton asked me to treat his daughter. He wanted Rae admitted as a patient at Inner Grace. Rae was totally against the idea. I went up to Ryce Hall to discuss the whole problem with Milton."

"What was the result of your discussions?"

A shrug accompanied, "Zilch."

"Was Rae present?"

"When I arrived on Friday night she'd just got there before me."

"Who else was present?"

Looking irritated to be asked, Edmundson said, "Verity was there for a few minutes, but said she had a headache and left. Apart from Rae, the roll call was me, Milton, Kym, and, of course, the diminutive Larry Frobisher, trolling for tidbits."

"You really don't like Mr. Frobisher, do you?"

"He's an obsequious, devious little man," he said disdainfully. "Some time ago he actually offered to pay me if I'd give him advance warning when I was admitting anyone famous to my clinic. When I told him to get lost in no uncertain terms, he had the audacity to approach some of my staff. I threatened legal action, and he backed off fast."

Thinking that she'd yet to come across someone who actually liked Larry Frobisher, except perhaps Ted Ryce, who seemed amused by him, Carol said, "Ted Ryce wasn't there?"

"Ted missed all the Friday night fun," Edmundson said with a sardonic smile. "He arrived early Saturday morning with Ian McNamara and a bunch of skydiving equipment. They had breakfast with us then went to unload stuff and put it into the Leapers Anonymous plane."

Carol leaned forward. "Did the equipment include the parachute packs for Milton Ryce and Verity Stuart?"

"I've no idea. I'm not interested in the sport. Seems idiotic to me to spend your time jumping out into a void." He grinned. "Not natural, is it? If God wanted us to fly, he'd have given us wings."

"If we can go back to the Friday night dinner," said Carol. "I believe you categorized it as a fun evening?"

"Sarcasm, Inspector. It was a debacle. Rae managed to turn what should have been a reasonably pleasant meal into a battleground. She argued bitterly with her father about what she called his 'fucking paternalism' among other choice epithets. The highlight of the evening occurred when Rae grabbed the edge of the tablecloth and yanked everything either into our laps or onto the floor. Predictably, she then stormed out. I presume she went back to Sydney."

"We've been told she's here at Inner Grace," said Carol.

Edmundson compressed his lips. "I told Rae not to call anyone. Who was it? Verity? Deanna?"

"This seems quite a reversal," said Carol. "On Friday night Rae Ryce is creating a scene and then storming off, presumably because she rejects her father's suggestion she become your patient. On Monday, here she is at your clinic. How do you account for that?"

"Rae changes her mind a dozen times a day. You can be a friend one minute, and an enemy the next. At the moment, she has me in the friendly camp."

"Have you admitted her as a patient?"

"The subject's off limits. I can't confirm—"

"I'll remind you again, Dr. Edmundson," said Carol coldly, "it's more than likely Milton Ryce was murdered. That makes this a murder investigation. Under the circumstances, you don't have the luxury of refusing to cooperate with the police."

"Rae's under sedation. She can't see you now."

"When can we interview her?"

Edmundson sighed. "First, let me say Rae's quite lucid, but naturally, very upset."

"You mean she's not under the influence of illegal drugs?"

He gave Carol a sour smile. "That is what I was subtly trying to point out. She had a mild sedative an hour ago. She's exhausted, physically and emotionally, so I'd expect her to sleep through until tomorrow morning. When she wakes, I'll tell Rae you want to see her."

"You're very protective of your patients?"

He looked surprised. "Of course."

"Was that why you threatened a citizen of Hash's Creek with legal action?"

Edmundson's face darkened. "I presume you're referring to Stevie Johnson. I heard him shooting his mouth off about Rae. It was slanderous. I told him so." He gave a short, acid laugh. "I don't know why I bothered, frankly. Rae's her own worst enemy. Gets herself into situations all the time."

"Why is that?"

A shrug. "Poor little rich girl syndrome, Inspector. Now, if there's nothing more . . ."

"I believe you had a disagreement with Basil Clement a few months ago. Was that also about Rae Ryce?"

Edmundson sat back in this chair. After a moment he said, "I accused Clement of supplying Rae with drugs. He took exception to that and hit me. I didn't have any hard evidence, just gossip, so I didn't take the matter further."

Carol rose to her feet. "Thank you for your time."

He picked up his phone. "I'll get Helen to see you out."

Helen Waite appeared within seconds, and stood waiting by the door.

"By the way, Dr. Edmundson," said Carol, "were you intending to tell us Rae Ryce was at the clinic?"

"I wouldn't have lied if you'd asked me directly."

"That's reassuring," said Carol. "One final point. I don't expect to have you tell me tomorrow morning that Rae has left the clinic without speaking to me."

He gave a sharp nod. "I understand you very well, Inspector. That won't happen if I can prevent it."

Helen led Carol and Anne to the entrance. "Good evening, Inspector Ashton, Constable Newsome." Then she waited rather pointedly for them to exit the building.

Once outside, Anne said with a grin, "I don't believe Ms. Waite likes us very much."

"She failed to protect her boss from us. That's why," said Carol, checking her messages. She'd set her cell phone to vibrate to avoid interrupting the interview with Edmundson. Someone—she was hoping Mark Bourke—had called just after she and Anne had been ushered into the doctor's office.

There was a voice mail from Bourke: "The guy from the safe

company had a hell of a time getting Ryce's safe open, but it was more than worth the trouble. Cash—looks like about half a million—two kilos of what I'm sure the lab will confirm is methamphetamine, and a smaller quantity of cocaine. We've hit the jackpot, Carol."

Chapter Ten

Carol waited until she got home before calling Bourke. When he came on the line, in the background she could hear a muted roar of conversation, dominated by Joycie's booming voice. "I'm in the dining room with Joycie as my dinner companion," said Bourke.

"I warned you, Mark. She fancies you."

Bourke chuckled. "Then don't leave me here too long, Carol. Pat won't forgive you if I succumb to temptation."

Grinning, Carol tried to visualize Joycie and Bourke romantically intertwined, but failed. "Is Joycie listening to your end of the conversation?"

"Absolutely. Hold on, I'll go outside."

A few moments later, the background noise had dissipated. "Okay," said Bourke, "I'm out on the veranda, and no one's near me."

"What's happened to the contents of the safe?"

"I've signed over custody to the district superintendent. He's arranging for everything to be transported, under guard, to Sydney."

"Who witnessed the opening?" Carol asked. With such a high-profile case, where everything would be scrutinized closely, it was vital there could be no opportunity to question the chain of evidence.

"Ron Dale, the safecracker, of course. And I had Huffner's sidekick, Constable Clive Whistler, with me. He witnessed the opening of the safe, and together we cataloged the contents and both signed off on the accuracy of the list."

"I'm surprised Sergeant Huffner didn't insist on attending," said Carol in a dry tone.

"Huffner tried mightily, but I pointed out how Hash's Creek needed his steady hand on the tiller. He wasn't impressed by this argument, so I got a bit firmer, and told him where he got off. Be warned, Carol. I gather he's intending to complain through official channels."

"Sergeant Huffner would be lucky to survive any close examination of his policing," said Carol acidly. "The more I hear, the more I believe he's corrupt. So far it seems to be petty stuff, like speeding tickets or looking the other way when influential citizens drink too much and then drive. Maybe I'm underestimating the good sergeant. Maybe he *is* into the big-time drug scene."

"Perhaps he is, peripherally. It took Ron so long to get the safe open, I got quite matey with Clive Whistler," said Bourke. "We traded stories—not always flattering—about our superiors."

"Thank you, Mark," said Carol with a laugh.

"It was all for a good purpose. With encouragement, he got quite expansive. It seems Huffner likes to boast he's particularly friendly with Basil Clement. It's Whistler's opinion Clement's just buttering up Huffner so he'll turn a blind eye to the wild parties Basil likes to throw."

"That's mild corruption, at the most."

"I think there's much more to it than that, Carol. Clement

made a fortune over the years on the golf circuit, but he spent a fortune, too. And now he's pouring millions into the house at Palm Beach he's building. Even with that drain on his resources, lately Basil Clement has been flush with cash, and spending it like there's no tomorrow."

"Drug money?" said Carol. "You're suggesting Huffner's in on it?"

"I think Huffner's being paid not to notice things, like late night flights into Ryce's airfield."

"And Milton Ryce had the combination for the safe. I don't imagine Ryce would just be storing the stuff for someone else. It's more likely he and Basil are in partnership."

"It's very possible," said Bourke. "I was going to ask Whistler if he'd heard anything along those lines, but just about then Ron got the safe open and all thoughts of anything else flew out of Whistler's head. After he'd exclaimed, 'Shit, look at that!' for the twentieth time I told him to shut up, and he took me literally. Besides, I could see Whistler was dying to get away and impress his friends with what he'd seen. I told him this was evidence in the investigation of Ryce's death, and he wasn't to breathe a word to anyone about what we'd found."

"So the cat's out of the bag," said Carol with world-weary cynicism.

Bourke snorted. "Out of the bag and talking nineteen to the dozen. I'd say half of Hash's Creek now knows what was in the safe."

"What about Ron Dale? Will he talk?"

"Ron? Hey, he's seen it all. Said I'd never believe what he'd found during his career of breaking into safes. He won't be saying anything, but it doesn't make any difference, now that law enforcement in Hash's Creek is in possession of the sensational facts."

"There'll be a media onslaught once this gets out," said Carol. "If anyone asks you for a statement, say a media conference will be held, but be vague about the timing."

"Ace reporter Yvonne Knight has already been badgering me,"

said Bourke with an indulgent laugh. "I keep on saying, 'No comment' to her. She isn't pleased."

Bourke undertook to e-mail Carol a full list of the safe's contents, mentioning that among the various business documents was a copy of Milton Ryce's last will and testament.

"Did you get a look at it?" Carol asked, keenly interested.

"A quick glance. The will's recent, it's signed and witnessed, and perhaps more to the point, it divides Ryce's estate exactly the way Larry Frobisher indicated. That is, apart from a substantial sum to medical research for children, half goes to the wife, Deanna, and a quarter each to his son and daughter."

"You haven't had a chance to chat up Polly Treeve yet, have you?"

"Not yet, Carol. I got her to invite me to have breakfast with her at Ryce Hall at some ungodly hour tomorrow morning."

"I knew Polly would be taken with your boyish charm."

"Let's see what I can get from her before you congratulate me. At least we won't have company to inhibit the conversation, as Bendix flew Ted back to Sydney this evening."

"What about Larry Frobisher and Kymberly Watson? Aren't they still at the Hall?"

"They've left, too, but by road. It was really quite amusing. In front of me, Frobisher asked Ted if he and Kymberly could catch a ride on the plane. I can give you Ted's reply verbatim. He looked Frobisher up and down, and said, 'Kym's welcome, but as for you, you freeloading little creep, you've got the last favor out of the Ryces you're ever going to get. Find your own way home.'"

"Oh, dear," said Carol. "Poor Larry. And here I was thinking Ted was just about the only one who had any liking for Frobisher at all. Any idea what turned Ted against him?"

"Not a clue. You must admit nobody seems to nurse much affection for the guy, although Kymberly Watson apparently drove to Hash's Creek with Frobisher on Friday afternoon, and still likes him enough to hitch a ride back to Sydney. I saw her loading her bags into his gargantuan four-wheel drive."

"When you speak with Polly Treeve, ask her if she knows anything about a defamation suit Ryce may have been bringing against Frobisher."

"I should think Larry Frobisher gets at least the threat of legal action every week," said Bourke. "His report cuts close to the bone. Who mentioned Ryce might sue?"

"Verity Stuart." Carol brought Bourke up to speed on that interview, as well as those she'd had with Deanna Ryce and Gilbert Edmundson. When she mentioned Rae Ryce's presence at the Inner Grace Clinic, Bourke said, "I've picked up a bit more information on Rae. Seems cocaine is her main drug of choice. Snorted, not injected."

"Yes, Mark, Dr. Edmundson confirmed the cocaine use."

"If it is cocaine in the smaller packet in the safe—and I'm almost positive it is—it looks to me like Daddy could have been her supplier."

"Or Ryce confiscated it from her and locked it away so she couldn't get at it."

"That's why they're making you Detective Chief Inspector," said Bourke with a laugh. "You're just so sharp!"

After she rang off from Bourke, Carol sank onto a stool in the kitchen and contemplated cooking something but felt too weary to bother. Sinker, her black-and-white cat, was giving her the feline cold shoulder because Carol had dared to be absent for one night and the best part of two days. Seating himself so that he gazed out the sliding glass doors leading to the deck, Sinker was behaving as though Carol didn't exist.

"You haven't got anything to complain about," she said to him. "You didn't starve, did you?"

Sinker all but snorted. Sure, the neighbor had provided him with food, but it wasn't the same, his furry back seemed to say.

A quick check of Carol's answering machine revealed only one message, left at seven p.m. It was from Lillian Broadhall, a friend of Aunt Sarah's and also an Eco-Crone of note. The message was short and to the point. In her usual succinct manner, Lillian gave her name, telephone number in the Blue Mountains, then said, "Sarah's party, Carol. Too much for you to handle solo. I'll coordinate. Crones provide food. And date change: Short notice, but has to be weekend after next. Will explain. Call back if before eleven. Or tomorrow morning, any time after six a.m."

Not being able to face talking to another person today, Carol decided to call Lillian in the morning. She got herself a chunk of cheese and some crackers, made a mug of coffee, and wandered into the sitting room to relax on the lounge and watch the late news.

Milton Ryce's death was still prominently featured, although the alleged satanic abuse of children in a suburban kindergarten had pushed it from the lead story. Carol watched Ryce's body thud into the ground for the umpteenth time, and wondered again what kind of son could sell this footage for profit. That led her to muse on Milton Ryce's family. Deanna appeared to despise her husband, Ted seemed barely touched by the tragedy, and Rae had clearly stated she was pleased her father was dead, although it was possible she was strung out on something when she said it.

If she had been under the influence of a drug, cocaine was the most likely candidate. A potent central nervous system stimulant, cocaine was powerfully addictive, but if Rae did use it, inhaling powder through the nose was marginally preferable to smoking crack cocaine or injecting the drug directly into the bloodstream. All three methods were dangerous, but crack smokers often suffered from acute respiratory problems, and needle users ran the very real risk of being infected with diseases such as hepatitis or AIDS.

Carol visualized Ryce's daughter as she had seen her in the paddock where her father had died. Cocaine was a stimulant, increasing temperature, heart rate and blood pressure. Users were often restless, irritable, anxious. That could describe Rae Ryce on Sunday, but it could also be the normal response of anyone to the violent death of someone close.

Looking back, it was curious how Rae's attitude had altered, once Carol had mentioned the possibility her father's death had not been an accident. Rae's angry hostility had abruptly changed to stunned shock, and then she'd hastily left.

If her shock were genuine, then Rae Ryce was no longer a suspect, because until Carol had mentioned foul play, Rae had believed Milton Ryce's death was an accident. After she'd so hastily fled from Carol and Bourke, where had she gone and why? To confront someone and accuse the person of murder? To warn someone? If the guard at Basil Clement's estate was correct, she hadn't arrived there until late afternoon. That left at least two hours unaccounted for.

Carol turned off the TV, picked up the phone and punched in Bourke's mobile number. This time the convivial sounds in the background were even louder. "You're in the bar, Mark?"

"I am Carol. Strictly research."

"Here's one thing more to add to the list. I want to know where Rae Ryce was in the two-hour window from the time she left us in the paddock until she turned up at the Clement place."

Carol disconnected, absently stroked Sinker, who'd apparently decided to forgive her, and mentally planned the next day. She'd take her usual early morning run, then call Lillian Broadhall. Then she'd contact Yancey Blake about borrowing Aunt Sarah's portrait. At work, she'd put Les Upton on the money trail, since he excelled at ferreting out financial details. Maureen Oatland could locate the Ryce chauffeur, Sandy Boyne, and then research past practical joke victims who could be possible suspects. Carol and Anne would interview Rae Ryce, if she hadn't disappeared from the clinic, and also Richie Keele, who'd been the subject of one of the most notorious of Milton Ryce's practical jokes. And there was Ian McNamara—the reputed lover of Milton's wife had to be interviewed, too.

Carol was suddenly swept with a desire to call Leota. Thanks to the International Date Line, the United States was the best part of a day behind Australia. It would be very early Sunday morning in Washington, D.C. She put her hand on the receiver, then took it off again. It was over, it was no use prolonging the parting. Leota wouldn't move permanently to Australia. Carol wouldn't relocate to America.

"I'm just feeling tired and lonely," she confided to Sinker. He gave her a wide, pink yawn.

"How right you are," said Carol, getting up. "Feeling sorry for yourself is very boring."

Carol rarely remembered more than fragmentary images from her dreams, but this time she experienced one so vividly tangible that when she woke she had to consciously persuade herself it *was* a dream, and not reality.

In her dream, Carol was lying naked on a tumbled bed in a moonlit room, filled with dark shadows. A draft of air lifted the curtains at the window, billowing them into silken sails. The breeze caressed her hot skin like the fingers of a lover, until she was consumed with a vast, incandescent desire—a sweet pain that swiftly grew until she writhed with its intensity.

Abruptly, she was aware she was no longer alone. A woman, wearing flowing robes, was standing in the shadows of the room. Carol couldn't see her face, yet somehow she was familiar.

The woman whispered Carol's name, a slow sibilant sound that jolted Carol with an even keener wave of longing. "Shall I come to you?"

"Yes," said Carol. "Yes!"

"Shut your eyes."

"No, I—"

"Shut your eyes."

Burning to see the woman's face, Carol hesitated, then complied. She heard the rustle of soft fabric, then felt a blindfold being gently tied about her head.

"Who are you?" Carol asked.

"You know."

Carol was about to protest that she didn't know, when the

woman's lips touched hers. A kiss that went on and on, a kiss that arched Carol's body until she quivered with yearning—not only for physical release, but for more, much more. For love, for understanding, for acceptance.

She turned her head to break the kiss and said, "Please . . ."

Somehow, Carol knew her unknown lover was smiling. The words Carol wanted to say broke up and sailed away as the woman's fingers found her center. Carol was plunged into a maelstrom. Had there ever been a lover like this, untiring, inexorable, unrelenting? Carol felt herself cresting. It was impossible to feel more. Yet she was driven higher, higher.

Sparks showered behind her closed eyes. Her body convulsed, vibrated. She heard herself cry out.

A wonderful lassitude flowed over her. Carol put up her hand to remove the blindfold, eager to see the face of the woman who had given her such pleasure.

But she was again in the shadows and moving away.

"Don't go."

"I must."

"But I don't know who you are."

The figure paused at the doorway. Before disappearing into the darkness, she whispered, "You do, Carol. You do."

A black wave of abandonment surged through Carol. Then she awoke.

Chapter Eleven

Lillian Broadhall answered her phone by crisply saying her name. Her tone indicated there had better be a good reason for the call.

"It's Carol. I got your message last night, but it was late, so I decided to call you this morning."

"Carol," said Lillian, her voice appreciably warmer, "you can relax about Sarah's party. Quite unreasonable to expect you to run everything. Providing your lovely house is enough. I'm coordinating. The Crones will do all catering, invitations and so on."

"In your message, you said something about a date change . . ."

"Quite so. Trust it suits you. Has to be weekend after next. Saturday night preferable. Must get e-mail invitations out quick smart."

Carol was used to Lillian's staccato delivery, and was often amused when she found herself imitating the clipped phrases. "Reason for date change?" she said.

"Crucial ecological conference in Brazil on global warming. Starts week of Sarah's birthday. As Eco-Crone president, imperative Sarah attend."

"That Saturday night will be fine, Lillian. Since you're coordinating, what can I do to help?"

Lillian assured Carol could do nothing but provide the venue, promised to e-mail a guest list for Carol to vet, and rang off with a terse "Goodbye now."

Carol, knowing her Aunt Sarah was invariably up with the dawn, punched in her number. "It's Carol. I've just spoken to Lillian about your party."

"Oh, darling," said her aunt, sounding quite subdued. "Lillian's read the riot act to me. And she's right. I shouldn't have demanded you give me a party without even asking you if you were willing to. Thank God the Crones are taking over, so you don't have to do all the work."

"Taking over is right!"

"Do you mind, Carol?"

"Mind? I'm delighted. And the earlier date is fine by me."

"Lillian's told you all about the conference in South America?"

"She snapped off a few short phrases about it."

Sounding considerably cheerier, Aunt Sarah said, "Imagine, darling, I'll be in Brazil. *Brazil*. And I'm to be one of the featured speakers at the conference! I'll be getting our Eco-Crones for the Environment message out to the whole world!"

"Aunt Sarah, that's wonderful."

"I'm already working on my speech, Carol. I was thinking of dressing as an endangered species to jazz it up. What do you think of that?"

Carol grinned. Having seen her aunt do street theater while colorfully costumed as a pesticide-contaminated butterfly, she was sure Aunt Sarah would go for maximum visual impact. "You certainly would be likely to get media attention," she said diplomatically.

"I knew you'd approve," said Aunt Sarah.

Carol had barely walked into her office and put down her brief-case before Lester Upton came in. "Two things. First, the lab left a message saying there are no usable fingerprints on the skydiving packs. As well, they had the results of the analysis of the packages found in Ryce's safe. The small one was pure cocaine. The other one contained methamphetamine." A rare smile appeared on his face. "You must have lit a fire under them. I've never known the lab to come in with results overnight, ever."

"Chalk it up to my winning personality. And what's the second thing, Les?"

"Someone called Sandy Boyne has been trying to reach you. I said you'd call him back. He says he has something of interest to tell you about the Milton Ryce case."

Les had been seconded to her team for a case some months ago, and she had kept him when a vacancy occurred. Carol certainly hadn't retained Les Upton for his sparkling wit. Though he wasn't bad looking, and physically trim, his impassive manner and mono-tone voice suggested a dull, rigid personality. It had been a surprise to Carol to find Les had a well-disguised dry wit. He was also incredibly tenacious and particularly skilled in following financial trails. Fine detail seemed to please him, and tedious tasks others groaned over invariably captured Les Upton's interest, so he showed as close to enthusiasm as he allowed himself when Carol asked him to investigate the financial side of the Ryce case.

When she called the number Upton had given her for Sandy Boyne, the phone was answered on the first ring. "Is that you, Inspector Ashton?"

"It is, Mr. Boyne. I believe you're anxious to speak with me."

"You could say that. I'm not far from the Police Centre. Do you want me to come in? I can be there in fifteen minutes."

"That would be very helpful."

When the chauffeur had rung off, Carol sat thinking about the contents of Ryce's safe. She called a friend in the drug squad, talked with him for a few moments, then sat tapping her pen absently on her desk. Morris and Basil Clement were the subject of an ongoing undercover operation targeting a web of drug distribution, and Milton Ryce was, as her friend in the drug squad had said sardonically, "A person of interest."

The smaller of the packets in the safe had held cocaine. Extracted from the leaves of the coca plant, most cocaine was smuggled into Australia, much of it originating in South America. Pure powder cocaine, as found in Ryce's safe, was often adulterated with other substances, such as talcum powder or even laundry detergent, before being sold on the street. The going rate varied from place to place, but sellers could expect to get around a hundred dollars a gram.

Methamphetamine, the other illicit drug found in the safe, presented a fast-growing threat in the club scene. Meth didn't have to be imported but could be cooked up in a makeshift lab by anyone with minimal training. Manufactured by combining a number of chemicals easily extracted from freely available products, including over-the-counter cold remedies, the resultant white crystalline powder had dramatic effects on the body.

Users experienced a jolt of energy and acute awareness, with an elevated body temperature. The drug decreased fatigue and dampened appetite. Highly addictive, meth's downside included hallucinations, paranoia and, in some people, out-of-control rages. Long-term users exhibited measurable brain damage, particularly to the areas controlling learning and memory. Meth addiction was notoriously hard to treat, having the lowest addiction recovery rate of any illegal drug.

Carol thought wryly that meth was the ideal illicit merchandise. Cheap and easy to manufacture locally, and highly addictive, it was an extremely profitable product. There were some problems: Meth labs used corrosive and toxic chemicals that could explode, so fires were common. The manufacturing process produced intense smells, almost impossible to hide. For every kilo of meth produced, five kilos of highly toxic waste was produced.

Les Upton knocked on her door. "Mr. Boyne's here."

Sandy Boyne was a short, stocky man with a shock of white hair. He had a small, pursed mouth, rosy cheeks and deep dimples, giving his face the look of a middle-aged cherub.

He strode into Carol's office, hand extended. Grabbing hers, he pumped it up and down. "Inspector Ashton! I've followed your career with interest. Bit of a buff on crime, you see." His accent was British, and Carol saw he wore a little Union Jack on the lapel of his jacket.

"It's very good of you to come in, Mr. Boyne."

"I saw it as my duty, don't you know?"

He took a seat, and looked expectantly at her. "Murder most foul," he said. "Ryce, I mean. Not some nasty mishap, but deliberate."

"You have some information for me, Mr. Boyne?"

"The wife fired me, I suppose you know that." At the thought, his cheeks grew redder. "Damn shame. Totally unwarranted. Just having a little chat with Bendix—you know the pilot, yes?—and happened to mention the McNamara chappie was unconscionably close to Mrs. Ryce. Bit of a scandal, what? Somehow she heard, and gave me my marching orders."

Deciding that the only way to get information out of him was to repeat the question until she got a straight answer, Carol said, "You were anxious to speak with me. Is there some information you have concerning Mr. Ryce's death?"

"Motive, my dear lady. Motive."

With the wry thought that, as far as Milton Ryce's death was concerned, motives were in plentiful supply, Carol said, "Yes, Mr. Boyne . . . ?"

"Working as chauffeur, one hears things. Odd isn't it, how people seem to think wearing a uniform makes one deaf?"

He paused, his expression expectant, clearly expecting some acknowledgment of his observation. When Carol nodded encouragement, Boyne went on, "Piecing bits together, Inspector, that's what happened. Not that I was deliberately listening, you understand, but bits and pieces came together."

Resisting a tart command to get to the point, Carol said, "I'd very much appreciate you telling me what you've surmised."

123

"*Surmised*. That's the word. Though perhaps *deduced* is more suitable . . ."

"Mr. Boyne!"

Sandy Boyne blinked at Carol's peremptory tone. "Oh, sorry, Inspector, I do tend to go on." Gathering his thoughts, he said with a rush, "You've met Mr. Clement? He was often a passenger, talking business with Mr. Ryce. And not all of that business was legal, Inspector."

"Could you be more precise?"

"Drugs. They had quite a partnership, dealing with illicit drugs."

"Basil Clement and Milton Ryce were partners in drug dealing?"

Boyne gazed at her, affronted. *"Basil?"* he said. "Where did you get that idea? It's *Morris* Clement I'm talking about."

Anne Newsome waylaid Carol on her way back to her office after seeing Sandy Boyne out. His information had been so diffuse, so much, as Boyne put it, "An impression, don't you know?" that Carol had decided not to take a formal statement from him at this time.

"Rae Ryce is champing at the bit," said Anne. "Helen Waite called from Inner Grace to say Dr. Edmundson thought we should know Rae is making I'm-getting-out-of-here noises."

"Okay, ring back and make sure Rae's still there. I'll meet you in the garage in five minutes."

Carol went back to her office to collect her things. On an impulse, she dialed Yancey Blake's number. "Yancey, it's Carol Ashton. How are you?"

"I'm fine, Carol, but I don't imagine you're calling to check on my health. What can I do for you?"

Carol pictured the woman on the other end of the line. Her most notable features were her piercing eyes. Carol put this down to the fact Yancey, as a portrait painter, automatically assessed every person she met as a possible subject. And then there was her thick, burnished brown hair.

Aware that by now Anne was probably waiting for her at the car, Carol succinctly explained why she wanted to borrow Aunt Sarah's portrait.

"No problem," said Yancey.

"And of course you're invited to the party."

"I don't think so, Carol. Sybil will be there, won't she?"

"I imagine so."

There was a pause, then Yancey said, "If it sounds like I'm avoiding her, it's true. I am."

"Yancey, I . . ." Carol stopped, not certain of what she wanted to say.

"It's entirely over, Carol. You know why."

Carol flashed back to the coffee shop a few months before, when Yancey, who'd arranged the meeting, had declared that Sybil had never got over Carol, and "for Sybil, anyone who isn't you, is second best."

Sybil had denied it, Yancey had said, but it was true, nevertheless. That was why Yancey was leaving the relationship.

At that point Carol had had an urgent call, and was forced to leave. She told no one of the conversation, and had pushed it out of her thoughts, at the time consumed with the decision of whether or not to join Leota in America.

"I'm sorry, Yancey," Carol said, meaning it.

"It's hardly your fault you're irresistible," said Yancey with an ironic laugh.

Assured that Rae Ryce was still in residence at Inner Grace, Anne drove the short distance to the clinic, while Carol recounted what Sandy Boyne had said about Morris Clement and Milton Ryce being partners in crime.

"Do you believe Boyne?" Anne asked.

"Mark found cocaine and meth in Ryce's safe, so I think we can assume Ryce was involved in some way with illicit drugs. As far as Morris Clement is concerned, perhaps it's true. Then again, maybe Boyne has some reason to set him up. Alternatively, Boyne could simply have put the wrong construction on what he overheard, and Morris is entirely innocent."

"I would have thought," said Anne, "Basil Clement would be the one to dabble in drugs."

"This isn't dabbling, Anne. The meth in the safe was worth a small fortune."

Anne swung into the Inner Grace driveway. Carol said, "When we interview Rae Ryce I want you involved. You're about her age, and she might answer your questions more freely."

Anne shot her an amused glance. "She's a lot more likely to answer *your* questions than mine, out of sheer respect."

"Deference for authority, Anne, is one thing Ms. Ryce does not possess."

Helen Waite was already at the door when they arrived, her expression less than welcoming. "Dr. Edmundson said to tell you Ms. Ryce has phoned for a taxi. It'll be here any moment."

"Cancel it."

"Inspector Ashton, I don't think—"

"Where is Rae Ryce?"

Her expression frigid, Helen Waite said, "In her suite, getting her things together."

"Please show us the way. We'll introduce ourselves."

She hesitated, then said, "Follow me, please."

Carol and Anne followed up a flight of stairs and down a corridor. Their feet sank into thick cream carpet. Flower arrangements were displayed in alcoves, and classical music played very softly.

Edmundson's assistant paused at a door, raised her fist and rapped gently. "Ms. Ryce? Are you there?"

From inside a muffled voice said, "The taxi's here already? Tell him I'll be a few minutes."

"Thank you, Ms. Waite," said Carol. "We'll take it from here." She opened the door and, Anne close behind her, stepped into a luxuriously appointed room.

Rae Ryce, startled, looked up from an overnight bag into which she was stuffing clothing. Her dark hair was disheveled and her face drawn. The diamond stud in her nose and the row of gold rings in one ear looked like tawdry window dressing, Carol thought.

Quickly regaining her equilibrium, Rae Ryce straightened up, saying, "You're the cop in the paddock where Dad died."

Carol held out her hand. "Inspector Carol Ashton, and this is Constable Anne Newsome."

Rae shook hands reluctantly. "You've caught me at a bad time. I'm just leaving."

"After you answer some questions," said Carol.

Anger flashed across the young woman's face. "You can't make me!"

"Ms. Ryce, your father's death was brutal. As he plunged toward the ground he would have been very aware there was no hope of survival."

Rae shuddered. "Dad was a bastard, but he didn't deserve to die that way."

Abruptly, all the bravado went out of her. She sank down on the edge of the bed, looking desperately weary. "Someone murdered him," she said.

"Who? Do you have any idea?" Anne asked.

Rae shook her head. "Plenty of people hated Dad, but not *that* much."

"Last Sunday," said Carol, "when I told you there were suspicious circumstances, and your father may not have died accidentally, you seemed very shaken."

Rae gave a rough laugh. "Shaken? Who wouldn't be?"

"Yet only a moment before, you were declaring how pleased you were your father was dead."

"I didn't mean it! You know how you say things in the heat of the moment . . ."

"You were angry with him?" Anne said.

Like a child, Rae pushed out her bottom lip. "He was always telling me what to do, threatening to cut off my allowance." She added resentfully, "And he was richer than God. Money meant nothing to Dad."

Carol moved to stand over Rae. "I told you it could be murder, and immediately you thought of someone, didn't you? That's what sent you rushing away."

Glaring up at her defiantly, Rae said, "I didn't rush away. I just left and went to Basil's place. Ask him, he'll tell you I stayed the night."

"Certainly he confirms you were there, Ms. Ryce. But there are two hours unaccounted for from the time you left the paddock and the time you turned up at the villa. Where were you?"

"I was upset. I just drove around, okay?"

"Did you call anyone?" Anne asked.

"It's my business what I did or didn't do." Rae Ryce got to her feet, and if Carol hadn't moved, would have shoved her out of the way. "I'm leaving. Don't try to stop me."

"Can you pack a parachute?" Carol asked.

Rae paused, her hand on the handle of her overnight bag. "Of course I can," she said disdainfully. "Dad made sure both Ted and I were expert skydivers. I took my first jump when I was just a kid."

"I've just got involved in the sport," said Anne in a friendly tone. "Only jumped in tandem, though. It'll be a while before I do it solo. I'm looking forward to it."

Rae shrugged. "The thrill wears off, believe me. I'm over it. I've found much more interesting things to do."

Carol was tempted to ask if one of those things might be cocaine, but not wanting to alienate Rae to the point where she would refuse to talk, said instead, "Ms. Ryce, please bear with us. You can imagine how difficult it is to investigate a case like this, where so many people have viable motives."

Releasing the handle of the overnight bag, Rae flung herself back onto the bed. "Shit," she said, "you can't think it's *me*. I've got an alibi. I was nowhere near Ryce Hall that Saturday."

"Alibis aren't much help in this case," said Carol. "Your father's gear could have been tampered with at any time before he leapt from the plane—in Sydney, or overnight at Hash's Creek. Even on the aircraft, it would be possible for someone to switch packs and give him a defective one."

Rae looked thoughtful. "Verity and Ian made the jump with him, so they were on the plane."

"So was Neville Bendix," said Carol.

"Bendix wouldn't have the guts," Rae declared emphatically. "Nor would Verity. But Ian's a different matter." She paused, head cocked. "Ian was fucking my stepmother—still is, I guess. Did you know that?"

Carol raised one eyebrow. "You're suggesting . . . ?"

"I'm not suggesting anything," said Rae, "although Dad dying is going to make Deanna awfully rich." She showed her teeth in a mirthless smile. "Isn't that every man's dream? To marry a rich widow? Ian's got it made."

The warmth of the morning and the thwack of balls coming from the private tennis court momentarily transported Carol back to her youth, when the endless days of summer had been taken up with tennis and swimming and just lazing around with her friends, soaking up the heat like young lizards.

Richie Keele's mother, a substantial, cheerful woman, had opened the door of the tennis star's sprawling home to Carol and Anne. "I'm Karen Keele. You're here to see Richie, of course. He's down at the court practicing with his coach. I won't lie to you. I've never been so pleased as when I heard Milton Ryce had plummeted into the ground. He deserved it. Does that make me a suspect, Inspector?"

"Mr. Ryce's death was not widely lamented, it seems."

Karen guffawed at Carol's dry tone. "Not widely lamented? That's good. I like it. Mind if I use it?"

"Be my guest."

The woman's face sobered. "That bastard," she said. "He all but ruined Richie's life. You know since the hoax, crowds taunt him at tournaments? Shout witticisms like the little green men are coming, or that Richie's opponent is fresh off a UFO."

"He must be very angry."

Karen Keele looked sharply at Carol. "Ridicule is a dreadful thing. It wounds the soul. Even so, Richie would never hurt anyone."

"This is just a procedural matter," said Carol soothingly. "We're interviewing many people who were associated with Milton Ryce."

"Associated with?" Karen Keele said darkly. "You mean, *victimized by*. I begged my son to sue Ryce, but he said it would just prolong his embarrassment by keeping the whole matter in the public eye."

She pointed out the way to the court, and left them with the final comment, "Frankly, I hope you never find out who did it, Inspector. The person did a service to humanity by eliminating that creature."

As Carol and Anne walked through lush gardens, Anne said, "His mother's right. Any legal action would just bring up everything again and remind people how gullible Keele was."

At the court, Richie Keele was practicing his serve, dispatching balls over the net with thunderbolt speed. Another man, presumably his coach, commented on each attempt, or stepped forward to make corrections to Keele's serving action. Carol and Anne watched for a few minutes, until Keele noticed them standing there.

Wiping his sweating face with a white towel, he came over to them. "Bloody hot," he said. "You're the cops, right?"

Assured that they were, he turned back to his coach, a tall man with a vaguely familiar face. Probably, Carol thought, a former tennis player on the circuit. Keele called out, "Bill, let's take a break. Fifteen minutes, okay?"

"You got it." The man began collecting the many tennis balls that littered the green surface of the court.

Richie Keele was lean and hard, his tanned legs corded with

muscle, his stomach flat. His arms were also well muscled, and Carol noticed his left arm notably better developed than his right, no doubt from years of thrashing a tennis ball left-handed.

Although only thirty, he was going bald, and like Mark Bourke, had chosen to minimize this with a very short haircut. In Keele's case he'd apparently shaved his head and let it grow back only to the point that it was a pale stubble on his skull.

Keele dropped into a chair and fished in a padded bag for a bottle of water. He threw back his head, took a long swallow, then said, "So what's this about? Ryce's dive into the ground?"

"You said some very bitter things about Milton Ryce."

"Too right I did! The bastard made me look like an idiot in front of millions of people. And worse, he single-handedly dealt a blow to support for SETI and similar organizations devoted to contacting other civilizations in the universe. I can't forgive him for that."

"When was the last time you saw Mr. Ryce?" Carol inquired.

"At the media conference where I was making a total idiot of myself in public, telling everyone how I'd seen a UFO, up close and personal."

Carol remembered how the media, conveniently ignoring the uncomfortable fact that they, too, had been fooled, had lapped up the shouting match that followed Ryce's revelation that Keele was the victim of an elaborate hoax. "You spoke to Milton Ryce after he'd revealed the truth, didn't you?"

Keele gave a bitter laugh. "Spoke to him? I'm sure you've seen the footage. I lost it. Made even a bigger joke of myself than I was already, by yelling every obscenity I could think of." He shook his head in disgust. "Played right into Ryce's hands. I couldn't have done anything more stupid, and it was just what he wanted me to do."

Carol noticed Anne's expression was sympathetic, and that she was unconsciously nodding agreement to Keele's conclusions.

"So it would be fair to say you nurse a grudge against the man?" Carol asked.

"Too right!"

"And you never approached him again, after that altercation?"

Keele grinned sardonically. "I'd learnt my lesson—keep away from the son of a bitch."

"Do you know any of Ryce's family or acquaintances?"

"No. And I don't want to." He paused. "I know Larry Frobisher, but then, everybody does. Frobisher wanted my first-hand account of what it was like to be the butt of one of Ryce's practical jokes. I told him to get lost, I wasn't giving interviews to anyone."

Anne frowned at him. "But you *did* give an interview to him, Mr. Keele. I remember it was the featured item on the Web site."

"Yeah, I did," he admitted, frowning in turn. "Frobisher talked me into it by saying how he, too, was Ryce's victim. Or at least, Ryce intended him to be the butt of a practical joke, but Frobisher said he'd found out about the scheme, and he was going to turn it around, so it blew up in Ryce's face."

"Have you any idea what stunt Ryce was going to pull?"

Keele shook his head, grinning. "Don't know, but I was waiting breathlessly to see the bastard get a dose of his own medicine."

The coach came over, and stood waiting, obviously expecting to resume the session. Carol said to Keele, "Have you any experience in skydiving?"

Keele's smile disappeared. "None. You won't get any crocodile tears from me. I'm glad that Ryce's dead, but I wouldn't know how to tamper with his parachute." He got to his feet. "If there's nothing more, I need to get back to work."

He picked up his racket. As a parting comment, he said, "I hope you don't find whoever it was, Inspector. They should be getting a medal for services to mankind, not being landed with a murder charge."

"Exactly his mother's attitude," said Anne as they left the court.

"I'm afraid it's shared by a lot of people. It's hard to find anyone who held Milton Ryce in high esteem."

Anne laughed. "Have you found a single person who does think well of him?"

"His son, perhaps. It'll make an interesting funeral ceremony. I suspect the crocodile tears Richie Keele mentioned will be flowing in abundance."

Bourke was on the road, driving back to Sydney. He called to report on his breakfast with Ryce's housekeeper. "Polly was quite forthcoming, Carol, once I'd laid the charm on with a trowel. Seems she didn't altogether approve of Milton Ryce's proclivities."

"And what proclivities would they be?"

"Polly delicately referred to them as 'Mr. Ryce's problem with women.' After more boyish smiles from me and a heartfelt compliment on her superb breakfast, she finally unbent enough to describe Ryce as a sex addict."

Carol raised her eyebrows. "She may be putting her own values into play here. One person's sex addiction is another's healthy sex drive."

"Polly insisted Ryce had a compulsion to bed every woman he came across. He didn't always succeed, but it wasn't for lack of trying."

"Don't tell me he tried it on Polly Treeve!"

Bourke's smile was indulgent. "I really like Polly, you know. She didn't beat around the bush, once she'd decided to tell all. Apparently years ago Ryce *did* put the hard word on her, after her husband died. Polly told him no, and that she was out of there if he ever suggested it again. He took her seriously. Never tried it a second time."

"Clearly a housekeeper is more valuable than a transitory satisfaction," said Carol dryly.

"Before you ask," said Bourke, "I did request a list of Ryce's conquests. It seems he was something of a sexual athlete, and Polly didn't pay much attention—it was just his way. She did confirm, however, a few people of interest."

"Kymberly Watson, of course."

"Kym was in a separate category. As Ryce's mistress, she was longer term. It was the short-term liaisons that had some eyebrow-raising names."

Bourke reeled off a list that included several women notable in

133

Sydney society. Others were the wives or daughters of Ryce's business associates.

"What about Verity Stuart?"

"She was there."

"Strange, she didn't mention it when I interviewed her," said Carol, grinning.

"And that defamation suit you mentioned, Carol? You were right on the money with that. The night before the jump, Frobisher and Ryce had a heated argument in the games room among all those toy soldiers. Polly came in with the whiskey nightcap Ryce had every evening, just in time to hear her employer shout at Frobisher that he'd take him for every cent he had."

"What had Larry Frobisher done?"

"As close as I can gather," said Bourke, "the Frobisher Report Web site was featuring a sensational item titled 'High Society's Nose Candy Crisis.' It was inferred that Rae Ryce, among others, was on the cocaine slippery slide to addiction hell."

"How did Larry Frobisher respond to Ryce's threat?"

Bourke laughed. "He tried, unsuccessfully, to placate the man. If I may quote Polly, 'Frobisher crawled like the sycophantic rodent he's always been.'"

"Sycophantic rodent?"

"Ah, Polly!" said Bourke. "She's a woman of many parts. She even had an answer to Rae's whereabouts for that two hours between leaving us at the death scene and lobbing in to stay with the Clement brothers."

"She went to Ryce Hall?"

"She rushed in, all agitated, demanding to know where Ted was. Polly said he was at the airfield, so Rae shot off again in that direction. Polly didn't see her again."

"Once Rae knew murder was on the cards, she had a burning desire to see her brother. What does that suggest to you?"

"That she suspected Ted was involved in some way."

"Hurry back, Mark," said Carol. "I need your man-to-man touch with Ted Ryce. I think he's due for another interview, don't you?"

Chapter Twelve

Back in her office, Carol fielded calls from the media, read a frame-by-frame analysis of the DVD containing the fatal jump—basically there was nothing of note—and skimmed through the post-mortem details. It was no surprise that Milton Ryce had died from extreme blunt force trauma. There had been no drugs in his system.

She had a copy of the DVD Ted Ryce had made, so she watched it again, interested this time in what came after Ryce plunged into the ground. At this point, Ted had turned the camcorder off. The next images were of Verity Stuart landing and tearing off her goggles and helmet. Ted had zoomed in on her contorted features as she stared, horrified, at Milton Ryce's body.

Then she struggled out of the straps holding her parachute pack and fell to her knees to throw up in the grass, each detail of her distress lovingly captured by the camcorder.

"You're a piece of work, Ted Ryce," said Carol to herself.

Summoned to the superintendent's office, Carol gave a brief

progress report, then returned to her office to listen to Les Upton enthuse about Milton Ryce's finances.

"Just preliminary stuff, but very interesting," said Upton, sitting down and leaning forward to fan papers across Carol's desk. "Financial statements from Ryce's company, bank records, philanthropic gifts and the like. Put some feelers out, and heard on the grapevine Taxation was after Ryce. That's no surprise. He had a lot of income unaccounted for, both in his company and in his personal accounts."

"It surprises me he'd be so careless," Carol remarked.

"Hubris," said Upton, shrugging. "These businessmen are convinced they're smarter than anyone else. They're wealthy and feel like nobody can touch them. Ryce made attempts to launder money, of course, but you need a really experienced accountant who specializes in dodgy deals to do it successfully."

Carol looked at the columns of numbers. They meant very little to her, but she'd found Les had an admirable ability to read them like a book. "It's probably drug money," she said. "Ryce had meth and cocaine in his safe."

"Yeah," said Upton, shaking his head, "that presents quite a problem. Cash flow is enormous in that business. You find yourself stashing money here, there and everywhere. A good move is to go into real estate with dummy partners, and to buy up businesses you can channel money through. Confuse the tax authorities. That's the name of the game."

"Was there a business partnership with Verity Stuart?"

Les flicked over several pages. "Yeah, look here. Renovating buildings in Woolloomooloo and Ashfield."

"*Two* projects?" said Carol. "Verity Stuart only mentioned one."

"Two, and a third in the works with Ryce funding it, like the others," said Les. "Financially, the Stuart woman's seriously overextended. She was lucky to have a money tree like Ryce backing her up."

"So what happens now he's dead?"

"I reckon she's on a frantic search for other backers."

Carol thanked Les for his good work, then mentioned the Clement brothers. "I've been told Morris Clement was a business partner of Ryce's in the illegal drug trade. And check out Basil Clement's finances, too."

"I'm on it!"

Amused, Carol watched Les Upton enthusiastically bounce out of her office. This was, she thought, certainly the most animated she'd seen him. She couldn't think of anything more boring than delving deep into financial matters, but Upton clearly found the assignment invigorating.

She called the number she had for Ted Ryce's Sydney address and got an answering machine. Without leaving a message she disconnected, then punched in Deanna Ryce's number. She hit the jackpot when Ted Ryce answered.

"Tracked me down, eh, Inspector?" he said cheerfully.

"I have some further questions. Would it be possible to see you tomorrow, Mr. Ryce?"

"Sorry, no can do. Up to my eyebrows in arrangements for Dad's service on Thursday. We're having a sort of wake afterwards. Dad would have liked that."

After Carol had made some appropriate comment, Ted went on, "Deanna tells me you're coming to the funeral. How about an invite to the wake, too? We can find time to have a chat then."

"That's very kind of you," said Carol, raising a mental eyebrow. It seemed Ted Ryce was providing her with an opportunity to see most of the suspects for his father's murder under one roof. She wondered why.

She snatched up the phone when it rang again. "Carol Ashton."

It was Vida Drake, a journalist noted for her ability to sniff out a story, run it to ground and shake it until the facts spilled out. "What's the word on Kymberly Watson?" she asked Carol.

"No comment, Vida."

"I believe you'd like to know the young woman is peddling her story around the traps. 'My hours of horror' seems to be her working title."

"She's entitled. It's a free country."

Vida snickered. "Not if you defame someone, it isn't."

"Who is she defaming?" Carol asked.

"Milton Ryce's wife, mainly, though she takes a swipe at the kids, Ted and Rae."

"So you're not touching the story?"

Vida laughed again. "Of course I am. Got the legal eagles going over it as we speak. I'd love to include a quote from you, Carol. Icing on the cake as it were."

"Sorry, Vida. Maybe later."

Shaking her head, Carol put down the phone. She'd seen it countless times, but it still sometimes surprised her the lengths to which people close to a victim would go in order to get some advantage for themselves.

She sighed when the phone rang again. "Carol Ashton." With a jolt she realized it was Sybil on the other end of the line.

"Carol, sorry to bother you, but Lillian Broadhall has given me a task for Aunt Sarah's party. She thinks a 'This Is Your Life' segment would go down well. Of course the guest of honor is to know nothing until we spring it on her in front of all the guests. Lillian's got plenty of material to do with Aunt Sarah's involvement in ecology and the Eco-Crones for the Environment, but she's got nothing much about her earlier life. I was wondering if you had anything I could use."

"I've got photo albums going back to when I was a kid. Lots of my aunt, I'm sure." On a sudden impulse, Carol said, "Are you doing anything tonight? We could go through the stuff together."

Sybil didn't immediately reply. Carol thought, *You're working out how to say no without seeming rude.*

Sybil said, "That's a terrific idea. What time?"

"Seven-thirty suit you? I'll order in pizza."

She'd put down the phone, and was staring into space, when Anne put her head through the door. "I got hold of Ian McNamara. He's coming in."

"Sit in on the interview, Anne."

Anne nodded, obviously pleased. Carol made a mental note to include Anne Newsome more often. It was so easy and comfortable to work with Mark Bourke, but Anne, who showed such great potential, should be challenged more.

"In fact, Anne, how about you start things off? Let's strategize, shall we?"

So many people had mentioned Ian McNamara that Carol found herself very curious to meet him. She checked through the little she knew of him. Ryce's company had been an important client for McNamara's business. More than one person had indicated he and Deanna Ryce were lovers. That didn't make it true, but Deanna had become agitated when McNamara's name had been raised. Carol recalled how Huffner had obviously been impressed by McNamara's icy cool demeanor at the death scene.

The man who was ushered into her office didn't fit Carol's mental picture. She'd pictured him tall and dark, with a cold, resolute face. In reality, McNamara was of medium height, with bright blue eyes, sandy hair going gray and what could truly be called an infectious smile.

"Delighted to meet you, Inspector."

Carol introduced Anne Newsome. McNamara was delighted to meet her, too.

He settled down amiably in a chair and waited for the first question. If he was surprised that it came from Anne, he didn't show it.

"You're a business associate of Mr. Ryce's?"

"Business and social. As I belong to Skydivers Anonymous, I often see him out of the office."

"The day he died—did you suspect something was wrong?"

McNamara tilted his head with a quizzical half-smile. "I'm not sure what you're asking, Constable."

"Was there anything out of the ordinary?"

"Not a thing. I arrived with Ted on Saturday morning, we

139

loaded the plane and took off for the drop zone. I remember Milton being in a particularly good mood, actually. Verity seemed very nervous, but she often was before a jump. And Bendix, the pilot, was pretty surly, but that was the norm for him."

"You jumped first?"

"I did. The plane went around, and then Milton went next. Verity last. It was a perfect day. I landed right on the bull's eye, so to speak, bundled up my chute, then joined Ted, who had his camcorder going."

Anne asked, "Was it usual for Ted to record jumps this way?"

That got a quick grin from McNamara. "Ted was usually on the camera when his father had something going."

"Meaning?"

"Meaning when Milton had some scheme to embarrass an innocent victim. This time I immediately realized it had to be Verity, since nothing untoward had happened to me. I remember I said to Ted, 'What are you up to?' but by this time he'd grasped something was wrong with his father's gear, and he didn't answer me."

"What happened then?"

"We both watched, horrified, as Milton hit the ground. There was no point in touching him. No one could have survived a fall like that. Kym got out of the Land Rover and came running over, screaming Milton's name the whole way."

"How did she know it was Ryce who'd fallen?" asked Anne. "She wasn't close enough to identify him, was she? From her point of view, couldn't it have been Verity Stuart?"

McNamara looked nonplussed for a moment, then his face cleared. "The jumpsuits, I imagine. They were both red, but from memory, Verity's had dark blue on it. Besides, Constable, anyone might scream, seeing someone plunge to their death that way."

"But she was screaming Milton's name, so she knew it was he who had died."

The first sign of irritation crossed McNamara's face. "I don't see it matters what Kym was screaming. The point was, Milton's life had been snuffed out a particularly ghastly manner. Anyone would be upset."

"But you were quite calm, weren't you?" said Carol.

He glanced at her, frowning. "That's how I react in emergencies. I shut down."

"Why did you call Dr. Edmundson?" Anne asked.

"Kym was hysterical. I thought she needed medical attention. And I was worried about Ted, of course. Having a doctor on the scene couldn't hurt."

"But Ted seemed okay, didn't he?" said Anne. "He continued to film Verity, even though his father had just died. That was the practical joke he was there to record—Verity's main chute had been disabled, giving her a terrible scare before her reserve chute opened."

"Yeah." His voiced was tinged with disgust. "Milton enjoyed upsetting people."

"We've been advised Milton Ryce played a practical joke on you some time ago," Anne said. "Is that true?"

Seeming relieved to be off the subject of Ryce's death, McNamara replied, "You mean the gun in the luggage? It wasn't a gun, of course, just the outline cut out of sheet metal. Frankly, I didn't find it funny, nor did the airport security people. And I told Milton so."

"And his response?"

McNamara made a face. "He told me I needed to develop my sense of humor."

"So in general you would say you were on good terms with Mr. Ryce?" Anne asked.

"Perfectly good terms."

"How about Deanna Ryce?" Carol interposed. "Were you on good terms with her?"

McNamara's smile blinked off as he swung his head to look at Carol. "We're friends," he said shortly.

"Close friends?"

His sandy eyebrows drawn down in a scowl, McNamara snapped, "It's Boyne, isn't it? Spreading unfounded rumors."

"Let me be very direct," said Carol. "More than one source has indicated you and Deanna are lovers."

He opened his mouth, then shut it again. Carol went on, "We've no interest in your private affairs, Mr. McNamara, except where they affect our investigation."

Ian McNamara's previously affable manner had completely disappeared. His face was hard, his eyes were narrowed. He got to his feet. "I've nothing more to say to you."

Carol stood. "We will have further questions. Constable Newsome, please show Mr. McNamara out."

When Anne came back Carol said, "Good work."

Anne glowed at the praise. "Thank you."

"Okay, Anne," said Carol, leaning back in her chair, "what would be your next move?"

"Interview Kymberly Watson again."

"Exactly," said Carol. "Set it up."

"Did you see that skydiving thriller, *Dropping Dead*, on TV last night?" Anne asked as she joined the traffic merging onto the Harbour Bridge roadway.

"No, I missed it," said Carol. "Would it have been good background for this case?"

"No way!" said Anne, laughing. "It repeated all the movie myths. First, the hero and his sidekick chatted happily with each other during free-fall—impossible, because the wind noise is so loud. Then the hero looks up, and horror! sees the villain has pitched the heroine out of the plane without a parachute. So naturally the hero catches her—like that'd happen at terminal velocity."

"You're destroying my illusions," Carol protested.

"There's more," said Anne. "The villain, with a mocking laugh, says, 'You forgot this!' and throws out the heroine's parachute pack, which, ignoring all the laws of physics, falls quickly enough for the hero to grab it. Can you guess what comes next?"

"I suppose the hero helps the heroine into the harness, they pull respective ripcords, and then, smiling, drift happily down together."

"You sure you didn't see it?" said Anne, grinning.

Fifteen minutes later, they were at the exclusive harborside apartment building where Ryce had installed his mistress.

Kymberly Watson's apartment was a lovely airy place, with a beguiling view of the tall city buildings, the Harbour Bridge and the Opera House. On the water, the constant movement of shipping, ferries and yachts had an almost hypnotic effect.

Although at their first meeting Kymberly had indicated she would have to relinquish the apartment almost immediately, since she would not be able to afford the rent, there was nothing to indicate a move was imminent.

Carol introduced Anne Newsome, who remarked, "A lovely place you have here, Ms. Watson."

Kymberly inclined her head in acknowledgment. "The view *is* beautiful, isn't it?"

She was far removed from the grief-stricken woman Carol and Bourke had interviewed at Hash's Creek. Her blue eyes were clear, her manner relaxed. Carol could appreciate what must have attracted Milton Ryce: long, blonde hair, a pretty face, a radiant smile, graceful movements and an excellent taste in clothes. Exposure to Kymberly's high-pitched little-girl voice would grate, Carol decided, but perhaps Ryce had found it charming.

Waving them to a white leather lounge placed to take best advantage of the harbor view, Kymberly said, "You mentioned, Inspector, there were a couple of matters you wanted to clear up?"

"Last Friday Milton Ryce drove up to Hash's Creek, instead of flying. That meant three hours on the road instead of minutes in a plane."

"Tell me about it," said Kymberly, grimacing. "*Totally* boring."

"But you weren't Mr. Ryce's passenger. You went with Lawrence Frobisher."

Looking even more disgusted, Kymberly said, "It was a setup. Milton insisted I hitch a ride with him. Larry was put out when he found there was no plane, but the little bastard cheered up when he discovered I was to be his passenger. I told Larry that Milton needed to talk business with Verity, so he'd suggested I ask Larry for a lift."

Intrigued, Carol said, "And the real reason for this was?"

"Milton had heard a rumor that Larry was preparing an expose for his Web site on cocaine use in high society, and that Rae was going to be prominently featured. Knowing how conceited Larry is, Milton figured it would be easy for me to get the truth out of him if we were stuck together for a long road trip."

"And was it?"

Kymberly gave a contemptuous snort. "Once he started talking, I couldn't shut Larry up. Then he realized he'd said too much, and begged me not to tell Milton anything about it. Just to stop Larry nagging me for the rest of the trip, I said I wouldn't breathe a word." She raised her eyebrows. "As if I'd keep anything from Milton!"

"And Mr. Ryce was angry when you told him the rumor was true?"

Kymberly smiled in reminiscence. "Absolutely furious. He said he'd bide his time, but that Larry Frobisher was going to pay dearly for his treachery."

"Mr. Ryce didn't say what he intended to do?"

She shook her head. "No, but I knew it would be nasty. No one crosses Milton and gets away with it."

"Does that include Deanna Ryce?"

When Kymberly didn't immediately reply, Anne looked up from her notebook. Carol waited a moment, then repeated the question.

"Milton was going to divorce his wife and marry me," Kymberly said defiantly. "Deanna would get nothing. He said his lawyers were making sure of that."

"Mr. Ryce said that he intended to marry you?"

Her face darkening, Kymberly snapped, "Is that so hard to believe?"

"No one else has mentioned the possibility."

"Well, of course not! It was a secret." She glared at Carol. "Anything else?"

"Who told you that Deanna Ryce had killed a man when she was a teenager in South Africa?"

A shrug. "I heard it somewhere."

"I'd advise you to cooperate," said Carol firmly. "You might find it preferable to being charged with extortion."

With an incredulous smile, Kymberly said, "Extortion? You're joking."

Carol regarded her coldly. This had the desired effect. "Oh, Christ," said Kymberly, "trust Deanna to take things the wrong way." She glanced at Carol hopefully. "I wasn't trying to get money out of her. She misunderstood. You know how that can happen."

"The source of the story?"

Kymberly sighed. "Milton. When he decided to divorce Deanna, he hired someone to dig up any dirt on her he could use. He was disappointed when the South African stuff was just about all there was."

"Thank you. It would have been far simpler if you'd told us that in the first place."

Appreciably relieved that the topic seemed finished, Kymberly belatedly offered refreshments. Carol declined.

"There were three people skydiving the day Mr. Ryce died," Carol said.

Kymberly frowned. "That's no mystery. Milton, Ian, and Verity went up in the plane with Bendix."

"When Sergeant Bourke and I interviewed you at Ryce Hall, you told us that, as Milton Ryce was plunging toward the ground, you screamed for him to open his parachute. Is that correct?"

"I'm not altogether sure what I said when you interviewed me—I was very upset. However, I do remember telling you something along those lines."

"Ian McNamara's recollection is that you were sitting in the Land Rover, and that you ran over, screaming Mr. Ryce's name, only after his body had landed."

A shadow of impatience crossed Kymberly's face. She spread her hands. "That morning was so confused and horrible. Everything's jumbled together in my mind. And anyway, what does it matter?"

"I am wondering," said Carol, "how you knew it was Milton Ryce."

"What do you mean?"

"Each person wore a jumpsuit, helmet and goggles, and all the parachutes were orange," Carol said. "Ian McNamara went first and landed safely. The aircraft went around and then the two remaining, Ryce and Verity Stuart, jumped, one after the other."

"So?"

"You say you saw someone falling, and realized something was wrong. But that person would just have been a dot in the sky. How could you be sure who it was?"

"What are you going on about?" she asked, her tone hostile.

"What I'm going on about, Ms. Watson," said Carol, "is the interesting fact that you seemed to know in advance who was going to die. It could have been Verity Stuart falling to her death, but by your own account you screamed out Mr. Ryce's name."

Kym put her hand to her mouth. "I've been trying to forget that awful moment." She gave a sob. "It's too upsetting."

Ignoring the threatened tears, Carol said, "Have you any explanation?"

Drawing herself up in injured dignity, she said, "You cannot possibly know, Inspector, what I've been through." Her lips trembled. "It embarrasses me to admit it, but it's possible I overdramatized things a little. Even though I wasn't sure it was Milton, maybe I called out his name—maybe I didn't. I'll never know for sure. Everything that happened that dreadful day is a blur to me now."

"It can't be *that* blurred," said Carol acerbically. "I believe you're selling your story to the media."

Her face hardening, she snapped, "There's no law to stop me, is there, Inspector?"

"In Australia the penalties for defamation are harsh."

"Deanna would never sue me," said Kymberly with conviction. "Everything I say will be the truth. That's a defense, isn't it?"

"And the truth is?"

"It's clear as the nose on your face. Deanna wanted Milton dead. With my own ears I heard her say those very words. And other people heard it, too. Now Milton *is* dead. Seems rather too much of a coincidence, don't you think?"

"By your own account, you've had experience in saying things you don't really mean. That could apply here," Carol said.

"Deanna meant it. Don't be fooled by that front she puts on. Underneath she's a Grade A bitch."

They discussed the interview as Anne drove back to the office. "What a bummer," Anne said. "I thought we'd caught Kymberly Watson out, because she knew beforehand Ryce would be the one plunging to the ground, but there's another explanation—she's a drama queen."

"It's certainly possible she's embellished everything later to sensationalize her moment in the limelight. Or it *was* a slip, and she did call out Ryce's name when she couldn't have known it was him. Realizing it's incriminating, she's covering herself by admitting she's over-dramatized the scene."

"And she accuses Deanna Ryce to take the heat off, by pointing us in another direction?"

"Kym Watson's had it in for Deanna from the beginning," said Carol.

"You can expect a mistress to dislike a wife, and vice versa. And in this case, the wife inherits millions, and the mistress gets nothing." Anne added with a grin, "That'd be enough to get me a little riled."

"Kymberly Watson strikes me as the sort who always knows which side her bread is buttered," said Carol. "She'd have encouraged Ryce to give her expensive jewelry, for example. And I imagine she's selling her story to the media, not giving it away."

"I reckon she's already working on a book," said Anne, laughing. "I can see the title: 'Murdered Millionaire's Mistress Tells All.' What do you think?"

"I think we'd better check who's paying her rent," said Carol.

Carol made it home earlier than usual. She smiled wryly to herself as she quickly tidied away newspapers, magazines and books. Who was she trying to impress? Sybil had lived with her for years and knew very well Carol's habit of always having something handy to read to fill any spare moment. And now that Carol was living alone, reading had become even more a solace.

Sybil arrived five minutes early. They had their usual uncomfortable moment at the front door, where neither one was quite sure how to greet the other. Carol surprised herself by giving Sybil a quick hug. Then, oddly embarrassed, she stepped back to allow her to enter the house they'd once shared.

Sinker, clearly pleased to see Sybil, came pacing down the hall, tail held high. "Sinker, you handsome cat, you!" she said. He graciously permitted her to stroke him, then set off toward the kitchen, looking back over his shoulder to give a plaintive meow.

"He hasn't changed," said Carol. "Food's still the way to his heart."

"Speaking of food," said Sybil, "do you mind if we order the pizza now? I missed lunch, and I'm starving."

Carol remembered she'd always had a healthy appetite, yet almost never gained weight. "I'll put the beer cans in the freezer to get them really cold, then while you call in the pizza order, I'll find the stuff on Aunt Sarah you want."

While Sybil was on the phone, Carol fed Sinker, then brought out the dusty photo albums she'd had stored away. She couldn't remember the last time she'd looked at them. "These go back forever," she said, stifling a sneeze.

Sybil had brought along a folder containing all the material Lillian Broadhall had provided. "Your aunt's been active in the

Eco-Crones for years," she said with a grin. She spread out press clippings on the kitchen bench. "Look at these. Aunt Sarah at the forefront, waxing militant."

"That's my aunt," said Carol with resigned pride.

Carol wiped the dust off the first photo album with a paper towel and plunked it down in front of Sybil. "This goes back eons. And don't laugh at any skinny blond kid you see—it's probably me."

Carol watched as Sybil bent her red head over the pages, bookmarking likely photographs of Aunt Sarah with strips of paper. She had beautiful hands, long-fingered and graceful.

"We had good times together, didn't we?"

The words were out before Carol realized she'd spoken her thoughts aloud.

Sybil looked up in surprise. The doorbell rang.

"I'll get it," said Carol, thinking, *saved by the pizza*. She'd act as if she'd never spoken, and the awkward moment would pass.

They cleared a space on the bench and perched on tall kitchen stools to eat. The beer was cold, the pizza wickedly decadent. They clinked cans in a silent toast, and just for a few moments, Carol felt at ease.

Sybil broke the mood by saying, "You've definitely decided not to move to the States?"

Was it definite? Carol thought. *Didn't Leota and I have something worth keeping?*

"I'm not moving to the States," she said, and for the very first time knew, unequivocally, that it was true.

Sybil nodded, but didn't comment.

Feeling the need to change the subject, Carol said, "I spoke with Yancey. She's happy to provide the portrait for the party."

"I presume you've invited her?"

"I did, but she refused."

Sybil winced. "Because of me?" Before Carol could say anything, she went on, "Of course, because of me."

Carol felt a sudden impulse to confess that Yancey had spoken

149

to her before the breakup, and had told Carol why it was happening. The urge to do so passed quickly. It would be betraying Yancey's confidence, wouldn't it? Or was that a rationalization to avoid hearing what Sybil might say in response?

"Coffee?" said Carol.

"Please."

With relief, Carol got up to fill her ancient percolator with ground coffee, and Sybil tidied up the remains of their impromptu meal. In an unspoken agreement, the topic of Yancey was dropped, as was any reference to Carol's decision to stay in Australia.

Soon the kitchen counter was stacked with photo albums, yellowed clippings and booklets. Carol picked up one of the booklets and flicked through it. 'Don't Kill Our Native Birds With Kindness' was the commanding title. It was one of many Aunt Sarah had run off on an old offset printing machine. When she was a kid, Carol remembered being pressed into service to collate and staple many copies of her aunt's authoritative words on various ecological matters, which would then be distributed to anyone willing to take the booklet.

"The titles got snappier as she went along," Carol remarked to Sybil. "Here's a more recent one."

The cover depicted the eighteenth hole of a golf course, with an expired bird, flat on its back, wearing a look of horror on its feathery face. Clutched in one claw was a little placard bearing the word: POISONED!

"I bet that title, 'Golf Courses Kill,' was a best-seller," Sybil said with a grin.

By the end of the evening Sybil had a pile of material to take back to her house. Carol packed it all into a box and sealed the top with tape.

"Carol, this has been a great help," said Sybil, preparing to leave.

Carol said, "Do you still feel the same about this house?"

Sybil looked at her for a long moment. "I'm afraid I do. I'm sorry. I know you love this place."

"I just wondered if time had made a difference."

"I'm much better," said Sybil. "I can stay here for an evening like this without having a flashback, but I don't ever want to push it. I know the house has been rebuilt, but it doesn't make a difference."

"I understand."

"Do you, Carol?"

"I really think I do." She picked up the box. "I'll help you out to the car."

It was a lovely night—a cloudless sky filled with stars and a soft breeze blowing. Sinker accompanied them halfway up the path to the street-level carport, then detected something lurking in the garden and went rushing away. "He's still a terrible hunter," said Carol, "so don't worry about him catching anything."

Carol slid the box onto the back seat. Another potentially awkward moment was broken when Sybil put a hand on Carol's arm and said, "Thank you, again," and got into the car.

Before she drove away, she put down the window. "We did have good times together, Carol," she said. "I treasure them."

Carol stood watching until the red taillights disappeared.

151

Chapter Thirteen

"I hope you don't mind me dropping in like this, Inspector Ashton."

"Not at all, Ms. Stuart." Carol ushered Verity Stuart to a chair. Today her long dark hair was pulled back in a chignon, and she wore a purple shirt with her white jeans.

Seated, Verity looked around Carol's office. "I can see my tax dollars aren't being wasted on luxurious furnishings."

Carol silently agreed. The kindest description of her office space would be *serviceable*. Averting her eyes from her in-tray, which was, as usual, overflowing, Carol jump-started the conversation with a brisk, "And how can I help you?"

"I've information I should have given you before."

"And that would be?"

Verity cleared her throat. "I don't want to say how I came upon this information."

Carol nodded. "Go on."

"Bendix was flying drugs for Basil Clement and his brother."

Sitting back in her chair, Carol said, "Indeed?"

"Do you believe me?"

With a faint smile, Carol said, "It would help to have hard evidence."

"Ask Huffner—Sergeant Huffner. He's in on it."

"You're saying Basil and Morris Clement are flying drugs in and out of Hash's Creek?"

"Out, mainly. The Clements have a meth lab set up in a trailer they've parked in a remote spot on their property. They package the drug in kilo lots and Bendix makes runs to Sydney and to selected country centers."

"How do you know this, Ms. Stuart?"

Verity shook her head. "I told you I wasn't going to say."

"Are you involved in this drug trade?" Carol inquired.

Her face filled with outrage, Verity snapped, "Absolutely not! Anyone who knows me is aware I'm totally anti-drugs."

"Then perhaps you'll tell me why you've come forward with this information now."

"Because it might have something to do with Milton's death. I think he stumbled on to what was happening, that his airfield was being used in a drug operation. I guess I'm saying that the Clement brothers had every reason to want to get rid of him."

Thinking of the drugs and money in Ryce's safe, Carol said, "So you don't believe Milton Ryce, himself, was involved?"

"Why would he be? He was rich. He didn't need the money."

In Carol's experience, where money was concerned, 'too much' rarely, if ever, applied. Rich though he might have been, Milton Ryce was unlikely to have refused money because he didn't need any more. Morality, though, was another matter. It was possible Ryce was opposed to the drug trade, specifically because his daughter was an addict. Ultimately, the drug squad investigation would settle the matter one way or the other.

"Did Mr. Ryce ever discuss drugs with you, on any level?"

"Our dealings were strictly business."

Carol raised an eyebrow. "Ms. Stuart, I must advise you that a witness has described your relationship with Mr. Ryce as being an intimate one."

Verity flushed. "Who said that?"

"Is it true?"

She moved uncomfortably on the chair. "It happened a few times." She looked defiantly at Carol. "On my part, it was a business decision. I needed the financial backing, and I was sure Milton would tire of me quickly. It wasn't much to endure, under the circumstances."

"And did he tire of you?"

"Oh, God, yes," said Verity. "Kymberly Watson came along and snatched him up. He didn't have a chance. Fucked him until his eyeballs bulged."

Hiding a smile at this description, Carol said, "So Ms. Watson did you a good turn?"

"Yes, but not on purpose. Kymberly only thinks of number one, a hundred percent of the time. She'd hooked Milton, and she was playing him like a fish on a line. She was aiming to get rid of Deanna and marry Milton herself."

"Do you think she would have succeeded?"

Verity gave a contemptuous laugh. "Kymberly had blown it by pushing too hard. That last day, Milton told me he was dumping her. 'Too high maintenance, too manipulative,' is what he said."

"But why would he confide in you?" Carol asked with a note of skepticism in her voice.

Verity smiled savagely. "He had a proposal. He was going to take up with me again—or so he thought."

"You wouldn't have been agreeable?"

"I'd have killed him first." She gave a half laugh. "Jesus, I don't mean that literally, Inspector. He was backing me financially. I wanted him very alive!"

Mark Bourke met Carol in the operations room where a white-board had been set up for the Ryce murder investigation. It was a utilitarian room. The walls were a grubby beige and the chairs and tables were mismatched and battered. Although often occupied with detectives listening with various levels of attention to brief-ings, at the moment the room held only Bourke and Carol.

"Verity Stuart is dead right about Huffner," said Bourke. "He's been suspended, pending an investigation. It looks like there's enough evidence to tie him to the Clements and Ryce. He was paid to turn a blind eye to the many flights in and out of Ryce's airfield, but he got greedy and tried for a bigger piece of the pie. If Ryce hadn't died when he did, I have a suspicion Sergeant Huffner would have met with a fatal accident himself."

"Can he implicate the Clements and Milton Ryce?"

"He's not talking at the moment, on legal advice. I'm sure that will change if he's offered a deal."

Bourke indicated his neat printing on the whiteboard. "Maureen's just reported to me on her investigations of other vic-tims of Ryce's practical jokes. None makes the short list of sus-pects. Every single person wished calamity to fall upon Milton Ryce, but no one had all the requisite points covered."

"Which are?" said Carol, peering at the board.

"Point one: the person or persons who killed Milton Ryce must have close familiarity with skydiving, or alternatively, be able to use the skills of someone who knows enough to sabotage Ryce's chutes.

"Point two: there has to be access, opportunity and enough time to fix the parachute pack that Milton Ryce intends to use, and it must be done skillfully, so nothing about his skydiving gear seems strange or out of place. Alternatively, the faulty pack is pre-pared long before, so it's ready to be switched at a convenient moment.

155

"Point three: a motive strong enough to trigger murder."

"Okay, Mark," said Carol, "if we rule out an unknown person with a grudge—and I think we can, because access to Ryce's equipment is vital—then who makes your short list?"

Bourke indicated the whiteboard. "The Clement brothers are at the top of the list. Drugs and money are a potent mix."

"If Morris Clement was in partnership with Ryce over illicit drugs," said Carol, "then why would he kill the very person who was providing organizational skills and the use of an airfield for distribution purposes? The same goes for his brother. Basil, of all people, can use the money. His lifestyle and grandiose architectural schemes would require constant injections of cash."

"Yes, but if Verity Stuart is telling the truth, the Clements have their own meth manufacturing unit going strong. Sure, it's convenient to use Ryce's airfield, but not essential."

"That's true," said Carol, "and greed is an excellent motive. Half the operation versus all of it. Morris and Basil could have decided it was worth the risk to eliminate Ryce and take everything for themselves."

"And there is that interesting point," said Bourke, "that Morris Clement volunteered for National Service, and became a military paratrooper, a fact he conveniently forgot to mention."

"Opportunity's a problem, unless someone with access to Ryce's stuff is an accomplice," said Carol.

Bourke grinned. "If you don't like the Clements, let me offer Ryce's nearest and dearest as possibilities. Ted and Rae both have that wonderful motive for murder—considerable financial gain. Rae has the added motive of hatred of her father. And both she and her brother know skydiving backwards."

Carol tapped the whiteboard where Deanna Ryce's name was printed. "And Deanna," said Carol, "has a very good reason to want her husband dead—the prenuptial agreement she's signed. If a divorce goes through, she gets very little; however, should Ryce die pre-divorce, she inherits millions. But she apparently knows nothing about skydiving."

"Ian McNamara does. And being Deanna's lover, he has every reason to want her to inherit, so he can share the fortune she'll be getting."

"To sum up," said Carol, "Ted and Rae are expert skydivers and could be expected to have free access to all Skydivers Anonymous equipment. Deanna claims to know nothing of the sport, but that's not a free pass, because Ian McNamara does, and he's in the plane with Milton Ryce, and could have switched packs."

"I'd much prefer Lawrence Frobisher to be the perp," said Bourke. "Inconveniently, he seems to know next to nothing about skydiving, but I'm sure he could have found an expert accomplice. And his motive's a good one—he's desperate to avoid Milton's defamation suit. Polly said Ryce was swearing to ruin him, and I reckon Ryce was the type to carry it through."

"Verity Stuart has opportunities galore, but no expertise in packing parachutes and no apparent motive. She didn't like Milton Ryce, but neither did most of the population, and it's not to her advantage to have him dead, as he's the one bankrolling her building makeover project in Woolloomooloo."

"After the trick he played on her, disabling her main parachute, I'd say she'd have killed him with her bare hands, if someone hadn't got to him first."

"Speaking of killing with bare hands, that would fit Richie Keele, wouldn't it? He's still being mocked for taking the UFO bait."

"Motive, but no opportunity or knowledge of skydiving."

"Unless," said Bourke with a grin, "he has an accomplice!"

"Kymberly Watson wouldn't need an accomplice. She has the knowledge and the access to Ryce's parachutes."

"So what's her motive?"

"On the face of it, she doesn't have one. Rather the reverse—she doesn't want to lose her meal ticket, so it's to her advantage to keep Ryce alive. But Verity Stuart says Ryce told her he was dumping Kymberly. If she knew that was about to happen, then I guess revenge becomes her motive."

"How about Bendix?" said Bourke. "He's got a cushy job, turning a blind eye to his employer's drug-running, and living in comfort on the property, with just a few aerial hops here and there to call work. What if he were inclined to try a little blackmail to cushion his old age? And Milton turned feral, as of course he would. Bendix then has a motive to get rid of his boss, and he also has plenty of opportunities to set it up."

"Too dangerous to even think of blackmail. Neville Bendix must have been aware how ruthless Ryce could be. Bendix might be amoral, but he's not stupid. I don't think he'd take the risk."

"Unless," said Bourke, "Bendix was doing it for someone else."

Carol rolled her eyes. "First we have an abundance of suspects. Now we have a plethora of accomplices. What a mess."

Anne came in to Carol's office, visibly excited. "Guess who's paid six months in advance on Kymberly Watson's apartment. Ted. Ted Ryce!"

"When did this happen?" Carol asked, looking up from the papers on her desk.

"A few days before Milton Ryce died."

"This little fact must have slipped Ms. Watson's mind when we last interviewed her," said Carol. "I wonder how Ted knew she was going to be available."

"Well," said Anne, "either Milton says to Ted, 'Son, I'm tired of Kym Watson—you can have her,' or, alternatively, Milton has no clue what's going on, but Ted knows his dad isn't going to be around all that much longer."

After Anne had left, Carol sat thoughtfully doodling on a scratch pad. Then she flipped open a file, checked a number and dialed.

"Mr. Keele? Inspector Ashton. I'd to clear up a couple of points."

After a short conversation, she thanked him, and disconnected. Then she went in search of Mark Bourke.

"Mark? What do you make of this? Larry Frobisher knew in advance that Milton Ryce was setting him up for a fall by arranging for the Frobisher Report to be leaked sensational, scandalous items. Each appeared to be genuine but was bogus. Frobisher told Richie Keele he discovered this by going through Ryce's desk at Ryce Hall—apparently an activity he indulged in frequently."

"It gives him an excellent motive. The Frobisher Report has got the clout it has because of his reputation for getting to the truth. Demonstrating he'd been sucked in completely would be devastating for Frobisher."

"He needs an accomplice, Mark. Frobisher hasn't the skill to disable the parachutes."

"Ted?" Bourke grinned. "Or Rae, or Kym, or McNamara? Take your pick."

"But not Verity Stuart?"

Bourke spread his hands. "Verity doesn't do parachutes, remember?"

"We'd better check that, Mark."

Chapter Fourteen

Milton Ryce had been nominally an Anglican, so his funeral was to be held in a fine old sandstone church more noted for celebrity weddings than final rites. It was a hot, sunny afternoon, the pale sky was cloudless, and cicadas trilled in the trees lining the street.

There'd been some talk of a symbolical skydiving event, with an empty parachute, appropriately weighted, drifting down to land nearby, but the authorities, citing public safety, had killed this idea, much to the disappointment of the television networks.

As Carol had expected, even without the empty parachute, this was a major media event. Television vans had claimed prime parking spots and reporters, both press and electronic, fought to seize the best positions to catch the stream of notable mourners entering the church. Crowds of curious onlookers pressed forward for a better view, some calling out to favorite celebrities, almost as though it were a movie premiere, with stars strolling down the red carpet.

Carol, wearing a classically tailored navy blue suit, stood unobtrusively to one side just inside the doorway, watching the arrivals. In the stream of solemn-faced people, the first Carol recognized was the deputy prime minister, who was there to represent the government. He garnered a few hoots from the crowd but maintained his usual unctuous expression. He was followed by Basil Clement in a dark charcoal suit of impeccable cut. Behind him, like a shadow, came Morris Clement.

As Basil reached the shallow sandstone steps at the entrance to the church, someone called out, "Good on you, Basil!" Smiling, Basil turned to wave. Then, apparently remembering the solemnity of the occasion, he assumed a grave expression.

Verity Stuart was next. She'd gone for high mourning, as if she were the widow herself. She'd chosen an outfit featuring floating panels in deep purple and black, topped off by a black hat and half veil.

Putting the lie to the widow's conviction that Kymberly Watson would not dare to attend the funeral, the next person Carol recognized was Kymberly herself, wearing a tight black dress and pressing a lace handkerchief to her lips. She walked slowly past the spectators and media people, pausing once or twice and turning a tragic face to the cameras.

Kymberly had only just disappeared inside when the main party of mourners arrived: Deanna Ryce, all in black, supported by Ian McNamara; Polly Treeve, stiffly upright; Rae Ryce, scowling as she strode along wearing three shades of black—polo shirt, jeans and sneakers; Ted Ryce, dark suit, red tie, his gait bouncy, his head turning from side to side as he checked out the crowd.

Hurrying to keep up with them, clearly uncomfortable in a suit and tie, was Neville Bendix. His lined face was solemn and to suit the occasion his luxuriant mustache seemed to droop more than usual.

Carol had arrived early, and had seen the casket, sleekly gleaming rosewood, carried into the church and placed on discreet supports in front of the chancel where everyone in the congregation could contemplate the brevity of life and the certainty of death. The funeral director had carefully positioned a gigantic bouquet of white lilies on top of the casket. Beautiful though the arrangement was, lilies were a flower Carol hated. She was never quite sure why, although she suspected it came from the profusion of lilies at both her mother's and father's funerals.

As she moved into the church, Larry Frobisher materialized beside her. "Here for the show, Inspector?"

"The show?"

"Where everyone pretends they're not absolutely delighted that Milton is dead and gone forever."

"That includes you, Mr. Frobisher?"

He ducked his head. "Not *me*, Inspector! I had a perfectly civil relationship with Milton."

"Indeed?" said Carol. "It's my understanding he was about to take legal action against you."

For a moment Frobisher seemed taken aback, then he said, "A vicious rumor, Inspector. I've had my share of those over the years."

"Mr. Ryce never played a practical joke on you, Mr. Frobisher?"

"No, of course not."

The organ music swelled. "I'd appreciate a word with you later," she said.

"At the wake, then, Inspector," said Frobisher, not entirely succeeding in looking nonchalant.

As Carol made her way to a pew, she noticed Ted Ryce was bending over his father's casket, apparently deep in prayer. Then, solemn-faced, he crossed himself, acknowledged the altar with an inclination of his head, and returned to the front pew where the rest of the family members were sitting.

Kymberly Watson had been bold enough to find a seat on the

other side of the aisle only a few rows back from the front. Head bowed, she was dabbing at her eyes with a lace handkerchief. Carol wondered cynically if this were entirely for show, or if she really did feel the grief she was displaying.

The solemn music faded to a whisper of sound that finally died away. It became so quiet that she could hear the rustle of clothes as people changed position, a stray word, someone's soft cough.

The officiating minister, hands folded in front of his vestments, face grave, opened his mouth to speak the first words of the funeral service. "We brought nothing into this world and it is certain we can carry nothing out. The Lord gave, and the Lord hath taken away; blessed be the—"

"Let me out! Let me out!" The thud of fists against wood seemed to be coming from the front of the church. "I'm trapped in here! I'm trapped in here! Let me out!"

The minister's mouth hung open; people were transfixed, eyes riveted on the polished casket. "Oh my God!" someone screamed. Kymberly Watson lurched into the aisle, hand to her mouth, then turned and bolted for the outside.

After the first jolt of surprise, Carol realized this had to be a hoax. She checked for cameras, and saw immediately that a television crew had appeared in a side aisle, and was recording the mourners' reactions.

She looked for Ted Ryce, and found him still in the front pew, gazing back at the congregation, an expression of smug satisfaction on his face. Their eyes met, and he smiled.

Carol got up and moved to the side aisle. The loud plea to be let out of the casket continued, the thumping of fists and the voice becoming more and more frantic.

Some mourners, obviously shocked, were standing, uncertain of what to do. Others remained seated, frozen. A few laughed, several were in tears. She checked out the mourners in the front pews. Rae Ryce was clearly furious, her glare hot enough to burn, had her brother cared to acknowledge it. Deanna Ryce's face was a frozen, pale oval. She sat stiffly, ignoring the consternation around her. Beside her, Ian McNamara had his head bent, resting his head on one hand, so Carol couldn't see his face.

One pew back, Basil and Morris Clement were a study in opposites. Basil, obviously shocked, was whipping his head around, as if seeking help. Beside him, untouched by the turmoil, Morris maintained his usual remote expression.

Further toward the back of the church, Carol saw Frobisher speaking rapidly into a mobile phone, his face alive with delighted amusement.

The officiating minister, bewildered, hadn't moved. Carol walked rapidly to the front of the church, paused at the first pew and said to Ted Ryce, "Turn it off, *now*," then went to the minister's side. "It's a hoax, reverend. Please calm everyone down."

He looked at her, dazed. "A hoax? Of course, a hoax."

Carol moved to the casket, certain that Ted had been planting a device when he'd apparently been deep in prayer over his father's body. She'd just located it, stuck to the underside of the casket, when the thumping and pleas to be released abruptly stopped.

She glanced back at Ted Ryce, who was grinning at her. He gave her a thumbs-up sign. It was obvious he wasn't at all uncomfortable about turning his father's funeral service into a fiasco.

The minister raised his voice, his sonorous tones rolling over the confusion. "People, please! This is the house of God. It's blasphemy to make a mockery of this service. Return to your seats, so the Order for the Burial of the Dead may resume."

Ted Ryce caught at her sleeve as Carol headed back to her place. "I did it for Dad," he said. He jerked his head in the direction of the vaulted ceiling. "He's up there, laughing, loving it."

Chapter Fifteen

Only the immediate family were to attend the burial in the Ryce family crypt. Other mourners made their way to the Ryce home in Turramurra. Carol had received an official invitation in the mail for: "A celebration of Milton Ryce's life."

She'd been forced to park some distance away, and enjoyed her walk through the tree-lined streets. On such an afternoon, the thought of death and decay seemed far away. Carol thought somberly how few people would be mourning Milton Ryce's demise with any sincerity. The function she was going to might be dubbed a celebration of Ryce's life, but Carol was keenly aware it was likely at least one person there would be silently celebrating his murder.

As she walked, she called Les Upton. "Les? What have you got for me?"

"Verity Stuart is a lucky woman." His voice was, for him, brimming with enthusiasm. "It seems no sooner had Ryce hit the ground than there were people lining up to finance her building proposals."

"Anyone of interest?"

"None of your suspects."

"That's a pity," said Carol.

"I left the best until last," said Upton. "These new backers? They all owe favors to Lawrence Frobisher."

Carol listened as he explained the situation in far more detail than she needed. When he ran out of steam, she asked Upton to transfer her to Anne Newsome.

Earlier, Carol had asked Anne where Anne would go if she wanted to be trained to pack a parachute. As Carol had suspected, certification was in the hands of the Australian Parachute Federation.

"I found her!" Anne's voice was exultant. "She was smart. She went north, out of the area, to an APF branch where no one would know her. But she had to use identification before she could enter the class, so there was a record."

Carol felt a surge of exhilaration. "Collect Mark and get up here, Anne. I don't want to give them time to get together to concoct a cover story."

Shortly after she'd joined the throng of guests helping themselves to the generous spread of food and drink set out under marquees in the rear garden, the members of the family funeral party arrived. Ted seemed subdued, Rae remote. Deanna looked drained, but anger animated her face. Beside her, Ian McNamara was speaking urgently, his hand on her arm.

Shaking him off, she raised her voice enough to be heard above the buzz of conversation. "Excuse me!" When silence fell, she went on in a voice choked with rage, "I must apologize for my stepson's disruption of my husband's funeral service. Ted had no right to subject you all to that disgusting display of so-called humor. I think it unlikely Ted will express regret, but I do so on his behalf."

166

Turning to Ted, she said, "Do you have anything to say to excuse your behavior?"

"I was carrying out Dad's wishes."

There was a murmur at this. Carol thought she was not the only one to find this a real possibility. It was the sort of thing Milton Ryce would have enjoyed.

Ted looked around, smiling. "My stepmother doesn't have a sense of humor," he said bitingly. "*I* do. I am my father's son. I saw it my duty to carry out his instructions. I'm content to think that he would be proud of me this day."

If Deanna had been angry before, now she was furious. Carol thought she would have struck Ted had not Ian McNamara forcibly led her away.

This contretemps had vastly entertained most of the guests. The noise level rose as people circulated around the tables spread with food. Carol located Frobisher in a knot of guests near the bar.

With a feeling of relief, she saw Mark Bourke and Anne Newsome appear at the edge of the crowd. Bourke gave her a quick nod. Deanna Ryce had been told what was happening.

"Inspector Ashton! You wanted to talk with me." It was Ted Ryce, still looking pleased with himself.

"Did Verity Stuart know her main parachute wouldn't open?"

Ted looked astonished. "Of course not. She wouldn't have jumped if she'd known."

"Are you sure?"

"Shit! It'd take guts. And Verity's a bit of a wuss, if you know what I mean."

"Did you know Larry Frobisher made it a habit to go through your father's desk at Ryce Hall?" Carol asked.

Ted scowled. "The little prick! I wasn't aware of it until I caught him going through the desk last Monday. And he still had the hide to ask for a seat in the plane back to Sydney. I told him where he got off."

"Your father kept meticulous records of his practical jokes."

Ted cocked his head. "He did, both in Sydney and at Ryce Hall. Why are you asking?"

167

"So Mr. Frobisher could have known that Verity Stuart was slated to be the next victim?"

Comprehension dawned on Ted Ryce's face. "Jesus Christ," he said. "Verity and Frobisher? I don't believe it!" He looked around the room and located Frobisher chatting with Neville Bendix. "The fucking little bastard," he said, half under his breath.

Carol said, "If you say or do anything, I'll arrest you for obstruction."

He put up his hands. "I won't say a thing."

Carol could see that Bourke was close to Frobisher. She searched the crowd and found Anne Newsome standing near Verity Stuart. She signaled to both of them.

She had to admire the way both Bourke and Anne dealt with their targets. Frobisher looked up at Bourke with indignation, then his shoulders slumped, and he allowed himself to be led away into the house. Anne was having an animated conversation with Verity Stuart, and apparently had come up with some convincing strategy, as Verity, still talking, walked with Anne through the back door.

Frobisher and Verity Stuart had been taken to separate rooms. Carol read the formal arrest first to Lawrence Frobisher. "I deny everything," he said. He glared at Bourke. "This is an outrage, arresting me at a function like this."

"A function to celebrate the life of the man you killed," Carol observed. "Or was it Verity Stuart's idea?"

"Yes! It was Verity. All I did was tell her Milton had sabotaged her main chute . . ." His voice trailed off.

"Thank you, Mr. Frobisher."

"I didn't mean . . ." He turned his head away. "I'm saying nothing more without legal representation."

When Carol went into the second room, she found Verity Stuart completely silent. The woman sat stone-faced as Carol read her rights. She was mute as Carol asked her whether she had switched Ryce's parachute pack on Friday night, after leaving the dinner with the excuse of a headache, or if she had waited until they were loading the plane the next day. Verity remained expressionless when Carol said that Lawrence Frobisher had already admitted warning her about the practical joke Ryce was going to play with the sabotaged parachute.

But when Anne led Verity Stuart out to the squad car, she looked back at Carol once, and there was burning rage in her eyes.

Driving back to the city alone, Carol mentally ran through the murder scenario. She was sure this was how it had gone down. Milton Ryce had alienated two people who would collude against him: Larry Frobisher and Verity Stuart.

Frobisher, snooping through Ryce's papers, had found that Ryce had plans to set Frobisher up as the next fall guy—a mortal blow to his pride, as all the time Frobisher had exulted in the thought he was a member of the inner circle and exempt from any of Milton Ryce's elaborate practical jokes. Frobisher also discovered that Verity Stuart was going to have a cruel trick played upon her. The next time she jumped, the main chute would be disabled, and she would spend what would seem an eternity in raw panic until her reserve chute came into play.

Frobisher told Verity what Ryce intended to do. She was murderously angry. Not only was Ryce having second thoughts about the projects she had mortgaged herself to the hilt for, he was asking sexual favors on one hand, and planning to scare the living daylights out of her on the other.

Frobisher approached Verity Stuart with a proposal. If she could find some way to disable the parachutes in an identical pack to the one Ryce would use, then switch it with Ryce's own carefully prepared equipment at the first opportunity, in return Frobisher would guarantee backers for her real estate projects by calling in favors owed to him.

No one could possibly suspect her, Frobisher pointed out, as who would believe she'd have the guts to jump, knowing one of her own parachutes was defective? And no one would suspect

Frobisher, because he had no familiarity with skydiving equipment at all.

To make sure she repacked the chutes properly, Verity took classes held by a APF branch. Using this knowledge, she sabotaged both chutes in a standard Leapers Anonymous pack and carefully repacked it so everything seemed okay. Then she waited for an opportunity.

Carol thought Ryce's final fatal step had been to threaten Frobisher with a defamation suit. She imagined he had gone straight to Verity's room at Ryce Hall to persuade her to go ahead with what seemed a foolproof plan. True, Verity would have to suffer the agony of knowing she was jumping with one disabled chute and that there was an outside possibility the other one might fail. But the mutual benefit was compelling. They would be rid of Milton Ryce, and both Verity and Frobisher would be in the clear.

No wonder Verity had vomited when she landed next to Milton's remains. She had screwed her courage to the breaking point to leap from a plane, knowing she would have to free-fall with only one parachute to stop her from plunging into the ground. What if it, too, had failed? Ryce's shattered body was demonstration enough.

Carol sighed. She'd thought herself hardened to all the dreadful things one person could do to another, but even she, with her long experience, could not imagine what it must be like to watch someone step confidently out into four thousand feet of empty air, knowing nothing would stop a headlong plunge to certain death.

Chapter Sixteen

It was three-thirty in the morning. The contingent of catering Eco-Crones had cleared up and departed and the last guest had finally drifted away, leaving behind a deeply pleased Aunt Sarah. Resplendent in the black-and-gold outfit she'd designed herself for the occasion—she decided not to depict an endangered species— her halo of white hair was still electric, but even her energetic self was wilting after so many hours of revelry.

Sybil, who had lingered to congratulate her, said, "You're a star, Aunt Sarah. I particularly liked the moment in your TV interview where you declared that the Eco-Crones would bring the board members of every rogue, polluting company to their collective knees. Good stuff!"

"Thank you," said Aunt Sarah, attempting to look modestly surprised at the praise.

Carol, back from farewelling the last person to leave, slumped in a chair. She felt simultaneously exhausted and exhilarated.

Everything had gone smoothly and obviously Aunt Sarah had had a wonderful time. The center of attention, she'd been at her bright, amusing best when giving the impromptu radio interview in the garden, which for the party had been strung with festive lights. The television crew had decided her portrait gave an excellent visual for the screen, so she'd been interviewed in front of that. Then there'd been a touch of drama when two media types got into a scuffle, which had given Carol an early opportunity to politely send all the media people packing.

"The whole evening went so well, darling," her aunt said, bending over to kiss Carol's cheek. "Thank you for everything."

"The Crones did most of the work," said Carol. "I just swanned around with the multitudes."

Aunt Sarah smothered a yawn. Glancing at the disarray in the living room, she said, "Can we finish clearing up in the morning?"

"It *is* the morning," Carol observed, "but I vote we worry about everything much, much later."

"A splendid plan." Aunt Sarah smothered another yawn. "I'm off to bed then." She paused to send a wicked smile in Sybil's direction. "You staying over, dear?"

Torn between amusement and irritation, Carol said, "Don't make trouble, Aunt."

"I'm just leaving," said Sybil. She gave Carol's aunt a warm hug. "A triumph, and well-deserved. Sleep well."

After Aunt Sarah had disappeared, Carol said affectionately, "My aunt never gives up, blast her."

Sybil gathered her things and Carol followed her out into the cool early morning air. A few sleepy birds were twittering, and the leaves of the gums whispered together. Other than those soft noises, there was a soothing hush lying over the world. Sinker, who'd disappeared for the night, suddenly materialized, and followed them up the path, his tail held high.

At the gate, Sybil turned back to look at the house. All the lights were still on, and it looked warm and welcoming. "I can see why you'd never leave this place, Carol."

Carol stood silently, regarding her home with a fond smile. In its several forms, it had been part of her life since her childhood. A movement caught her attention. A curtain was billowing in the casual breeze.

Without looking at Sybil, Carol said, "We could buy something together."

She was aware Sybil was staring at her. "Carol? What do you mean?"

Absurdly nervous, Carol linked her fingers in Sybil's. If Sybil drew away, Carol felt the moment would be lost forever. Sybil didn't move.

Still gazing down at the lighted windows, Carol said, "Just a thought. We sell our houses, and use the money to buy something that would be ours—not yours or mine."

Silence. Carol said, "I'm holding my breath, so say something, anything, before I run out of air."

"You really mean it?"

"I really mean it."

Carol turned to face her. "You don't have to say anything now." She released Sybil's fingers. "But I wish you would."

"This is quite a shock."

"I feel that way, too," said Carol with a half-smile. "I'd no idea I was going to say it . . . And mean it."

Sybil looked steadily at her, frowning slightly.

"I believe," Sybil said, "I could become accustomed to the idea."

About the Author

Claire McNab is the author of fifteen Detective Inspector Carol Ashton mysteries: *Lessons in Murder, Fatal Reunion, Death Down Under, Cop Out, Dead Certain, Body Guard, Double Bluff, Inner Circle, Chain Letter, Past Due, Set Up, Under Suspicion, Death Club, Accidental Murder* and *Blood Link.* She has written two romances, *Under the Southern Cross* and *Silent Heart,* and has co-authored a self-help book, *The Loving Lesbian,* with Sharon Gedan. She is the author of five Denise Cleever thrillers, *Murder Undercover, Death Understood, Out of Sight, Recognition Factor,* and *Death by Death.*

An Australian now living permanently in Los Angeles, she teaches fiction writing in the UCLA Extension Writers' Program. She makes it a point to return once a year to Australia to refresh her Aussie accent.

Publications from
BELLA BOOKS, INC.
The best in contemporary lesbian fiction

P.O. Box 10543, Tallahassee, FL 32302
Phone: 800-729-4992
www.bellabooks.com

SUGAR by Karin Kallmaker. 240 pp. Three women want sugar from Sugar, who can't make up her mind. ISBN 1-59493-001-5 $12.95

FALL GUY by Claire McNab. 200 pp. 16th Detective Inspector Carol Ashton Mystery. ISBN 1-59493-000-7 $12.95

ONE SUMMER NIGHT by Gerri Hill. 232 pp. Johanna swore to never fall in love again—but then she met the charming Kelly . . . ISBN 1-59493-007-4 $12.95

TALK OF THE TOWN TOO by Saxon Bennett. 181 pp. Second in the series about wild and fun loving friends. ISBN 1-931513-77-5 $12.95

LOVE SPEAKS HER NAME by Laura DeHart Young. 170 pp. Love and friendship, desire and intrigue, spark this exciting sequel to *Forever and the Night*. ISBN 1-59493-002-3 $12.95

TO HAVE AND TO HOLD by Peggy J. Herring. 184 pp. By finally letting down her defenses, will Dorian be opening herself to a devastating betrayal? ISBN 1-59493-005-8 $12.95

WILD THINGS by Karin Kallmaker. 228 pp. Dutiful daughter Faith has met the perfect man. There's just one problem: she's in love with his sister. ISBN 1-931513-64-3 $12.95

SHARED WINDS by Kenna White. 216 pp. Can Emma rebuild more than just Lanny's marina? ISBN 1-59493-006-6 $12.95

THE UNKNOWN MILE by Jaime Clevenger. 253 pp. Kelly's world is getting more and more complicated every moment. ISBN 1-931513-57-0 $12.95

TREASURED PAST by Linda Hill. 189 pp. A shared passion for antiques leads to love. ISBN 1-59493-003-1 $12.95

SIERRA CITY by Gerri Hill. 284 pp. Chris and Jesse cannot deny their growing attraction . . . ISBN 1-931513-98-8 $12.95

ALL THE WRONG PLACES by Karin Kallmaker. 174 pp. Sex and the single girl—Brandy is looking for love and usually she finds it. Karin Kallmaker's first *After Dark* erotic novel. ISBN 1-931513-76-7 $12.95

WHEN THE CORPSE LIES A Motor City Thriller by Therese Szymanski. 328 pp. Butch bad-girl Brett Higgins is used to waking up next to beautiful women she hardly knows. Problem is, this one's dead. ISBN 1-931513-74-0 $12.95

GUARDED HEARTS by Hannah Rickard. 240 pp. Someone's reminding Alyssa about her secret past, and then she becomes the suspect in a series of burglaries.
ISBN 1-931513-99-6 $12.95

ONCE MORE WITH FEELING by Peggy J. Herring. 184 pp. Lighthearted, loving, romantic adventure.
ISBN 1-931513-60-0 $12.95

TANGLED AND DARK A Brenda Strange Mystery by Patty G. Henderson. 240 pp. When investigating a local death, Brenda finds two possible killers—one diagnosed with Multiple Personality Disorder.
ISBN 1-931513-75-9 $12.95

WHITE LACE AND PROMISES by Peggy J. Herring. 240 pp. Maxine and Betina realize sex may not be the most important thing in their lives.
ISBN 1-931513-73-2 $12.95

UNFORGETTABLE by Karin Kallmaker. 288 pp. Can Rett find love with the cheerleader who broke her heart so many years ago?
ISBN 1-931513-63-5 $12.95

HIGHER GROUND by Saxon Bennett. 280 pp. A delightfully complex reflection of the successful, high society lives of a small group of women.
ISBN 1-931513-69-4 $12.95

LAST CALL A Detective Franco Mystery by Baxter Clare. 240 pp. Frank overlooks all else to try to solve a cold case of two murdered children . . .
ISBN 1-931513-70-8 $12.95

ONCE UPON A DYKE: NEW EXPLOITS OF FAIRY-TALE LESBIANS by Karin Kallmaker, Julia Watts, Barbara Johnson & Therese Szymanski. 320 pp. You've never read fairy tales like these before! From Bella After Dark.
ISBN 1-931513-71-6 $14.95

FINEST KIND OF LOVE by Diana Tremain Braund. 224 pp. Can Molly and Carolyn stop clashing long enough to see beyond their differences?
ISBN 1-931513-68-6 $12.95

DREAM LOVER by Lyn Denison. 188 pp. A soft, sensuous, romantic fantasy.
ISBN 1-931513-96-1 $12.95

NEVER SAY NEVER by Linda Hill. 224 pp. A classic love story . . . where rules aren't the only things broken.
ISBN 1-931513-67-8 $12.95

PAINTED MOON by Karin Kallmaker. 214 pp. Stranded together in a snowbound cabin, Jackie and Leah's lives will never be the same.
ISBN 1-931513-53-8 $12.95

WIZARD OF ISIS by Jean Stewart. 240 pp. Fifth in the exciting Isis series.
ISBN 1-931513-71-4 $12.95

WOMAN IN THE MIRROR by Jackie Calhoun. 216 pp. Josey learns to love again, while her niece is learning to love women for the first time.
ISBN 1-931513-78-3 $12.95

SUBSTITUTE FOR LOVE by Karin Kallmaker. 200 pp. When Holly and Reyna meet the combination adds up to pure passion. But what about tomorrow?
ISBN 1-931513-62-7 $12.95

GULF BREEZE by Gerri Hill. 288 pp. Could Carly really be the woman Pat has always been searching for?
ISBN 1-931513-97-X $12.95

THE TOMSTOWN INCIDENT by Penny Hayes. 184 pp. Caught between two worlds, Eloise must make a decision that will change her life forever.
ISBN 1-931513-56-2 $12.95

MAKING UP FOR LOST TIME by Karin Kallmaker. 240 pp. Discover delicious recipes for romance by the undisputed mistress.
ISBN 1-931513-61-9 $12.95

THE WAY LIFE SHOULD BE by Diana Tremain Braund. 173 pp. With which woman will Jennifer find the true meaning of love?
ISBN 1-931513-66-X $12.95

BACK TO BASICS: A BUTCH/FEMME ANTHOLOGY edited by Therese Szymanski—from Bella After Dark. 324 pp.
ISBN 1-931513-35-X $14.95

SURVIVAL OF LOVE by Frankie J. Jones. 236 pp. What will Jody do when she falls in love with her best friend's daughter?   ISBN 1-931513-55-4 $12.95

LESSONS IN MURDER by Claire McNab. 184 pp. 1st Detective Inspector Carol Ashton Mystery.   ISBN 1-931513-65-1 $12.95

DEATH BY DEATH by Claire McNab. 167 pp. 5th Denise Cleever Thriller.
                                                        ISBN 1-931513-34-1 $12.95

CAUGHT IN THE NET by Jessica Thomas. 188 pp. A wickedly observant story of mystery, danger, and love in Provincetown.   ISBN 1-931513-54-6 $12.95

DREAMS FOUND by Lyn Denison. Australian Riley embarks on a journey to meet her birth mother . . . and gains not just a family, but the love of her life.   ISBN 1-931513-58-9 $12.95

A MOMENT'S INDISCRETION by Peggy J. Herring. 154 pp. Jackie is torn between her better judgment and the overwhelming attraction she feels for Valerie.
                                                        ISBN 1-931513-59-7 $12.95

IN EVERY PORT by Karin Kallmaker. 224 pp. Jessica has a woman in every port. Will meeting Cat change all that?   ISBN 1-931513-36-8 $12.95

TOUCHWOOD by Karin Kallmaker. 240 pp. Rayann loves Louisa. Louisa loves Rayann. Can the decades between their ages keep them apart?   ISBN 1-931513-37-6 $12.95

WATERMARK by Karin Kallmaker. 248 pp. Teresa wants a future with a woman whose heart has been frozen by loss. Sequel to *Touchwood*.   ISBN 1-931513-38-4 $12.95

EMBRACE IN MOTION by Karin Kallmaker. 240 pp. Has Sarah found lust or love?
                                                        ISBN 1-931513-39-2 $12.95

ONE DEGREE OF SEPARATION by Karin Kallmaker. 232 pp. Sizzling small town romance between Marian, the town librarian, and the new girl from the big city.
                                                        ISBN 1-931513-30-9 $12.95

CRY HAVOC A Detective Franco Mystery by Baxter Clare. 240 pp. A dead hustler with a headless rooster in his lap sends Lt. L.A. Franco headfirst against Mother Love.
                                                        ISBN 1-931513931-7 $12.95

DISTANT THUNDER by Peggy J. Herring. 294 pp. Bankrobbing drifter Cordy awakens strange new feelings in Leo in this romantic tale set in the Old West.
                                                        ISBN 1-931513-28-7 $12.95

COP OUT by Claire McNab. 216 pp. 4th Detective Inspector Carol Ashton Mystery.
                                                        ISBN 1-931513-29-5 $12.95

BLOOD LINK by Claire McNab. 159 pp. 15th Detective Inspector Carol Ashton Mystery. Is Carol unwittingly playing into a deadly plan?   ISBN 1-931513-27-9 $12.95

TALK OF THE TOWN by Saxon Bennett. 239 pp. With enough beer, barbecue and B.S., anything is possible!   ISBN 1-931513-18-X $12.95

MAYBE NEXT TIME by Karin Kallmaker. 256 pp. Sabrina has everything she ever wanted—except Jorie.   ISBN 1-931513-26-0 $12.95

WHEN GOOD GIRLS GO BAD: A Motor City Thriller by Therese Szymanski. 230 pp. Brett, Randi, and Allie join forces to stop a serial killer.   ISBN 1-931513-11-2 $12.95

A DAY TOO LONG: A Helen Black Mystery by Pat Welch. 328 pp. This time Helen's fate is in her own hands.   ISBN 1-931513-22-8 $12.95

THE RED LINE OF YARMALD by Diana Rivers. 256 pp. The Hadra's only hope lies in a magical red line . . . climactic sequel to *Clouds of War.*   ISBN 1-931513-23-6 $12.95

OUTSIDE THE FLOCK by Jackie Calhoun. 224 pp. Jo embraces her new love and life.
ISBN 1-931513-13-9 $12.95

LEGACY OF LOVE by Marianne K. Martin. 224 pp. Read the whole Sage Bristo story.
ISBN 1-931513-15-5 $12.95

STREET RULES: A Detective Franco Mystery by Baxter Clare. 304 pp. Gritty, fast-paced mystery with compelling Detective L.A. Franco   ISBN 1-931513-14-7 $12.95

RECOGNITION FACTOR: 4th Denise Cleever Thriller by Claire McNab. 176 pp. Denise Cleever tracks a notorious terrorist to America.   ISBN 1-931513-24-4 $12.95

NORA AND LIZ by Nancy Garden. 296 pp. Lesbian romance by the author of *Annie on My Mind*.   ISBN 1931513-20-1 $12.95

MIDAS TOUCH by Frankie J. Jones. 208 pp. Sandra had everything but love.
ISBN 1-931513-21-X $12.95

BEYOND ALL REASON by Peggy J. Herring. 240 pp. A romance hotter than Texas.
ISBN 1-9513-25-2 $12.95

ACCIDENTAL MURDER: 14th Detective Inspector Carol Ashton Mystery by Claire McNab. 208 pp. Carol Ashton tracks an elusive killer.   ISBN 1-931513-16-3 $12.95

SEEDS OF FIRE: Tunnel of Light Trilogy, Book 2 by Karin Kallmaker writing as Laura Adams. 274 pp. In Autumn's dreams no one is who they seem. ISBN 1-931513-19-8 $12.95

DRIFTING AT THE BOTTOM OF THE WORLD by Auden Bailey. 288 pp. Beautifully written first novel set in Antarctica.   ISBN 1-931513-17-1 $12.95

CLOUDS OF WAR by Diana Rivers. 288 pp. Women unite to defend Zelindar!
ISBN 1-931513-12-0 $12.95

DEATHS OF JOCASTA: 2nd Micky Knight Mystery by J.M. Redmann. 408 pp. Sexy and intriguing Lambda Literary Award-nominated mystery.   ISBN 1-931513-10-4 $12.95

LOVE IN THE BALANCE by Marianne K. Martin. 256 pp. The classic lesbian love story, back in print!   ISBN 1-931513-08-2 $12.95

THE COMFORT OF STRANGERS by Peggy J. Herring. 272 pp. Lela's work was her passion . . . until now.   ISBN 1-931513-09-0 $12.95

WHEN EVIL CHANGES FACE: A Motor City Thriller by Therese Szymanski. 240 pp. Brett Higgins is back in another heart-pounding thriller.   ISBN 0-9677753-3-7 $11.95

CHICKEN by Paula Martinac. 208 pp. Lynn finds that the only thing harder than being in a lesbian relationship is ending one.   ISBN 1-931513-07-4 $11.95

TAMARACK CREEK by Jackie Calhoun. 208 pp. An intriguing story of love and danger.
ISBN 1-931513-06-6 $11.95

DEATH BY THE RIVERSIDE: 1st Micky Knight Mystery by J.M. Redmann. 320 pp. Finally back in print, the book that launched the Lambda Literary Award–winning Micky Knight mystery series.   ISBN 1-931513-05-8 $11.95

EIGHTH DAY: A Cassidy James Mystery by Kate Calloway. 272 pp. In the eighth install-ment of the Cassidy James mystery series, Cassidy goes undercover at a camp for troubled teens.   ISBN 1-931513-04-X $11.95

MIRRORS by Marianne K. Martin. 208 pp. Jean Carson and Shayna Bradley fight for a future together.   ISBN 1-931513-02-3 $11.95